Coronation

NOVELS BY
PAUL GALLICO

The Snow Goose
The Lonely
Jennie
Trial by Terror
The Small Miracle
Snowflake
The Foolish Immortals
Love of Seven Dolls
Ludmila
Thomasina
Flowers for Mrs Harris
Mrs Harris Goes to New York
Too Many Ghosts
Confessions of a Storyteller
Scruffy
Coronation

NON-FICTION

The Steadfast Man: A Life of St Patrick
The Hurricane Story

PAUL GALLICO

CORONATION

HEINEMANN

LONDON MELBOURNE TORONTO

William Heinemann Ltd

LONDON MELBOURNE TORONTO

CAPE TOWN AUCKLAND

THE HAGUE

First published 1962
Reprinted 1962

© Copyright 1962 by Paul Gallico

Printed in Great Britain
by The Windmill Press Ltd
Kingswood, Surrey

FOR MY GOD-DAUGHTER
LAURA LEGH

The wheels of the Coronation Special from Sheffield, due at St Pancras Station at six o'clock in the morning of Coronation Day, 2 June 1953, sang the steady, lulling dickety-clax, dickety-clax of the British Railways. Approaching a crossing, the engine shrieked hysterically into the drizzly night as it pulled its heavy load through the countryside, London-bound. In the third-class compartment occupied by the five members of the Clagg family and three other passengers, no one slept, though Granny kept nagging at the two children to try to do so because of the long exciting day ahead.

True, the crotchety gentleman in the bowler hat in the corner was trying to doze against odds. He had taken the window seat craved by eleven-year-old Johnny Clagg, the elder of the two children. Johnny had wished to sit there so that trying to see through the grimy, rain-streaked window-pane he might, with his active and ambitious imagination, project himself adventuring through the darkness. The occasional stab of a car headlight from nearby roads led him to transform himself into the daring dispatch rider carrying the message through enemy lines that would save the regiment. He kept pushing over almost on to the lap of the man, the better to visualise himself in the pitch blackness, hurtling through a hail of enemy bullets. Every so often his mother pulled him back with, 'Now, Johnny, don't push the gentleman who's trying to sleep.'

Johnny sighed and obeyed. Always the grown-ups, either Mum or Granny, were shattering the pictures of his imaginings when they were at their most exciting.

His sister Gwendoline, who was seven, was turning the pages of a souvenir Coronation booklet containing photographs of the queen who was to be crowned that day.

The child was wearing her best dress, now slightly too small, even though let down. Mrs Clagg had braided red, white and blue ribbons into her two ash-blonde pigtails and the added touch of colour lent an astonishing felicity to her appearance. She was elfin rather than pretty, with her mother's large pale eyes and eyebrows and her father's firm chin.

Gwendoline was obsessed with Queen Elizabeth the Second. For weeks, as the day of the Coronation approached, she had filled her waking thoughts and sometimes her dreams at night as well, and in one of these she had been held in her arms and cuddled. When she woke up she had lain there remembering the wonderful dream, the soft white robe worn by the Queen, the butterfly crown upon her head; in one hand she had carried a wand with a star on the end of it and had smelled of some heavenly scent.

Despite the sickly yellow light of the dimmed compartment lamps Gwenny continued to stare, fascinated as ever by the frontispiece photograph in the booklet. Every so often she would lean down and press her cheek to that of the image of the smiling, tiara-crowned Queen on the smooth surface of the glossy paper, and whisper to it, 'I love you.'

It was not that the child was starved for affection, for Violet Clagg was a loving and warm-hearted, if perpetually weary and over-worked mother. It was rather that in Gwendoline's mind a picture had been formed of a bright, exquisitely beautiful and glamorous super-mother.

Illustrators of children's stories and fairy tales sometimes succeed in appealing directly to the heart of a child and providing it with an image that in one form or another lasts throughout a lifetime. Such a figure for Gwendoline had been the Butterfly Princess, a pale gossamer girl who in one of her books reigned over the butterflies. And at night in her bed in the before-going-to-sleep fantasies Gwendoline would go to her.

Lately Gwenny had found a new love, the Queen. Something in all the hundreds of photographs of her that she saw – the tiny figure, the smile, the calm, grave eyes – touched her heart. The Queen was a real, living person. The Butterfly Princess was a coloured drawing in a picture-book. In the process that only children know of, fairy princess and Queen blended into one and Gwenny's secret being turned towards her as a flower twists upon its stem and lifts its face to the sun. Now she was on her way to keep a rendezvous with her.

3

The child raised her face from the booklet and asked for reassurance again that it could actually be so. She seized her mother's arm. 'Am I really going to see her? Will she be able to see me too?'

With the practised disinterest and the automatic reaction of mothers who have learned to cope with more than one child, Violet Clagg replied, 'That's right, dearie,' without at all interrupting her own train of thought, which at that moment was centred upon the vision of a bottle of champagne wrapped in a white napkin being served by a liveried butler. She was seeing herself holding a thin-stemmed glass in her hand, her little finger elegantly crooked. The yellow wine was about to bubble forth.

'But how close, Mummy? How really close?'

Violet Clagg struggled against her daughter's insistence as she did against all insistences, those of her mother, Granny Bonner, and her husband, as well as the even more strident demands of modern life with none of which she seemed to be able to cope. She was a plain, friendly-looking, put-upon person, worn with work.

Moving pictures and blatantly coloured advertisements in the women's magazines brought her to the doorstep of glamour and luxury, yet never once had it been permitted her to cross the threshold, at least never until this adventure upon which they were now embarked. Very little in her life had ever come up to expectations, so that she had become confirmed in the apathy of disappointment. She hardly could believe that the pattern was about to be broken. And yet she was indeed seated in a train bound for London, to see crowds and people and flags and bands and beautiful dresses, jewels and tiaras and the crowned Queen of England, and drink bubbly out of a special glass.

'*How* close, Mummy?'

She succumbed. 'Well, now, as close almost maybe as your daddy. You can wave to her like this—' She picked up her daughter's hand and dipped it across the carriage at Will Clagg, her husband. He was explaining to an elderly draper from Salford and his wife how they had managed to acquire five seats in a window on Wellington Crescent near Hyde Park Corner, the best place of all to see the procession, for here it turned into Wellington Place after marching down Piccadilly and swerved again to enter the East Carriage Drive in the Park, so you really saw it twice.

'My cousin Bert in London got them for me,' he was saying. 'We had seats in a stand in mind, but he's got connections. Works for a big car-hire firm.'

Granny Bonner, Mrs Clagg's mother, prototype of all grannies – iron-grey hair collected in a bun, alert, shifting critical eyes behind steel-rimmed spectacles, thin, dried-up, disapproving mouth – had to put in her twopenn'orth as she always did when Bert was mentioned. He was, of course, Will's cousin and thus from the wrong side of the family: 'I wouldn't know much about Bert's connections. He only washes the cars.'

5

Will Clagg glared. He was a stocky but bulkily muscular man, a figure appropriate to the foreman in charge of the No. 2 furnace at the Pudney Steel Works, Great Pudney, on the outskirts of Sheffield. His dark Sunday suit and mackintosh made him look even lumpier, but for all of his powerful frame, dark hair and his bristle of moustache, there was something engaging about him and a kind of permanent innocence seated in his blue eyes. 'He got 'em for us, didn't he?' he said, and reached a hand to the inside pocket of his coat to feel their presence. 'Like to have a look at them?' he asked.

As always when he produced the tickets the entire family, even Granny Bonner, became electrified and crowded closer to view their blue and gold majesty. Johnny returned from the black night without. He had exchanged his motor-cycle for a tank and had been standing in the turret directing its move-up for a dawn attack. Granny hitched around in her seat and looked over her spectacles. Violet Clagg endured the almost insupportable sweetness of pride and happiness mingling in her bosom. Even Gwenny emerged for a moment from her preoccupation with the pictures of the Queen.

'Here they are,' Will Clagg said, proudly extracting them from his wallet and handing one to his neighbour.

It was of stiff, azure blue cardboard. The printing thereon was gold-embossed over a large 'E II R' worked into the centre. It read: 'Coronation Procession 2 June 1953. Admit one to No. 4 Wellington Crescent, Hyde

Park Corner, S.W.1. Window One. Row A. Seat 1.'
Further advice to be found upon it was that it was non-transferable; that the price was twenty-five guineas, breakfast at eight and midday buffet lunch with champagne included; and finally, it stated that the premises had been leased by the Victoria Coronation Co. Ltd., 18 Victoria Road, S.W.1.

The draper was impressed, not only by the elegance of the ticket but the price. He said, 'Twenty-five guineas! Dear me, that's a lot of money.' Some quick mental arithmetic was even more impressive. One hundred and twenty-five guineas – perhaps two whole months' wages for the foreman of a mill.

The sound of 'twenty-five guineas' caused the bowler hat type in the corner seat to open his eyes and sit blinking at the pasteboards in Clagg's hands. Clagg, however, was suddenly looking as horrified as though he had been suspected of robbing the Bank of England. 'We didn't *pay* all that for 'em,' he protested. 'Good Lor', no. Bert got 'em for ten quid apiece through one of his connections.'

In spite of the fact that she was dazzled by the tickets, Granny couldn't help putting in, 'I'd like to see some of Bert's connections some time,' causing Clagg again to hustle to his defence: 'Maybe you will when we're in London. There'll probably be some of the bigwigs right where we'll be sitting.'

The man in the corner, who had the hook nose and pop eyes of a parrot, pulled himself together and suddenly held out his hand for a ticket. It appeared at first that somebody at some time or another had tried to sell him a gold brick or he was just naturally suspicious, for he gave the thing as thorough an examination as he could without splitting it. He scrutinised both sides, held it up to the carriage light, and even for an instant with a somewhat grimy finger-nail scratched at the gold of the lettering, causing Clagg to cry out with alarm, 'Here, don't do that!'

The man, not at all put out, looked at the minute fleck of gold attached now to the finger-nail and, having completed this investigation, he handed it back remarking, 'First-class stuff. That's a pretty good job. I'm in the printing trade myself.'

Everyone sighed with relief. Clagg found himself holding the tickets and running his own stubby fingers over the comforting embossing. 'Would you like to look?' he asked the draper and his wife.

They each took one and marvelled, not only at all that the tickets implied but also the bargain involved. Violet Clagg said, 'Imagine seeing the Queen *that* close as she goes by in her golden carriage! The kiddies will have something to tell *their* kiddies, won't they? And a drink of real champagne to go with it!'

The draper's wife said, 'I envy you. It will be something to remember. I think it's wonderful that you've managed it so that all of you could go.'

'Ah now,' said Will Clagg proudly, 'that's when you've got the kind of family like mine. We put it to a vote.

8

"Annual hols. at Morecambe or go to London for the Coronation," I said. "One or the other. Can't do both. All those in favour!" It was four to one for the Coronation.'

'I only said it seemed like squandering money,' Granny snapped, thus answering the question in the minds of the listeners as to who had vetoed the proposition, 'when the children ought to be having their two weeks by the sea.'

'We talked her into it,' Will Clagg said good-humouredly, winking at his wife.

The draper's wife said, 'Oh, but surely you're glad now that you're going?'

Granny wasn't going to give in that easily. 'That's to be seen,' she said testily.

Clagg laughed. 'When Granny here gets to heaven,' he said, 'she won't believe it until the angels show her their wings are growing and not stuck on!'

For an instant behind her spectacles Granny's little eyes screwed up in an expression as close to hatred as she was capable of assuming. She didn't like to be reminded of heaven or, if not heaven, then dissolution, which was for her now an ever-present eventuality. She was seventy-three and of course subject to those notifications and warnings delivered by weight of years – a twinge here, a creaking, an unexplained ache or pain. Yet the alarms these set off in her mind were real enough. Three score years and ten was the allotted span, She had exceeded it by three, and in one sense considered herself flying in the face of the Bible. Granny was filled with an insatiable curiosity as to what the next day would bring, besides which there were Johnny and Gwendoline growing up and needing her to instil the old-fashioned virtues. Bossing was her life.

Everyone smiled at Granny in a friendly and amused manner at Clagg's joke, for all of them had at one time or another known old ladies like that, and none of them guessed that she was both angry at and frightened of the word 'heaven'. Carefully, almost tenderly, Clagg restored the tickets to his pocket.

No man in the United Kingdom would have been more upset, astonished and incredulous than Will Clagg had he been told that the reason he had gathered up his family and journeyed to London for the Coronation was that he was in love with the Queen of England.

He was not alone in this. Not since the time of Elizabeth the First had such a surge of chivalrous passion swept through the hearts of the men of Great Britain as on this Coronation Day. Modern times or no, the young man in the bowler hat, the countryman in his boots, the labourer in his overalls, each had felt the all-encompassing sweep of mediaeval woman-worship, the *Domnei* of the troubadors. All England and the Commonwealth too were united in a gigantic, emotional love affair with their Queen-to-be-crowned. It had merely engaged Will Clagg a little sooner.

It had come to him, as a matter of fact, at the passing of the late King, when he had seen a picture of her in the newspapers upon her swift and sudden return from Africa.

She had been photographed hesitating a moment as she descended the steps of the aircraft, and she was seen thus, a tiny and forlorn figure in black, over the backs of her Ministers ranged before her in their sombre clothing like crows lined up on a pole. She had left the country as a gay young Princess and she was returning a saddened Queen. Clagg had looked upon the picture long and silently and felt his heart go out to her.

She had asked all of her subjects to pray for her at that time. Outwardly Clagg was neither emotional nor demonstrative, nor what one would have called a religious man. No one would ever know that he had done as the Queen had requested and that night had thought a silent prayer for her, a simple one in which he asked something or someone whose name was God, without being at all able to conceive what this God was like, to help the Queen, to save and keep her. But from that moment on he was bound to her, and the journey to London was something very ancient in his blood, a drawing of himself as a loyal subject to the foot of the throne, a gesture, a fealty and a courtesy as well.

But as for the manner of expressing his emotions, or rather turning them into action, Clagg was all artlessness and directness itself. He simply said, one Sunday afternoon early in April at the dinner table of their semi-detached house at No. 52 Imperial Road, Little Pudney, 'Look here, what would you say to all of us going to London for the Coronation?'

The query had shattered, staggered, uplifted, hypnotised, terrified and enthralled his family. He had thrown it on to the table like a live fuse, where it burned and sputtered, throwing out the smoke and flame of adventure.

Not that they weren't already Coronation-minded; the newspapers and magazines had been full of it for months with articles and photographs, and the tension and excitement was already beginning to mount and spread to the farthest corner of the United Kingdom and across the seas to the Commonwealth.

Violet Clagg was the first to react to the glory that had been proffered, the prospect so rich, so glamorous and so deeply craved by her person starved for change and excitement. She echoed his words: 'Go to London! For the Coronation! All of us? Oh, Will!' And the depth of her desire was expressed in the way she spoke the last two words. But thereafter all of the old fears and frustrations and disappointments took over. 'But we couldn't manage standing in the street with the children all night. They couldn't possibly.' For there had already been stories that people were planning to reserve places by the kerbside where the procession would pass by establishing squatters' rights and sleeping there for nights before.

Johnny had cried, 'Who'd care? I could see the soldiers!'

Violet continued, as though anxious as quickly as possible to voice all of the things against: 'And Mother's too ol . . . I mean, her feet swell when she stands.'

'Bother my feet!' Granny had snapped. 'Do you want

the children to catch their death of cold? What if it rains? You want them sitting out there all night catching pneumonia? You must be out of your mind, Will Clagg.'

'No, no, no!' Will had shouted. 'You never let a man get in a word in his own house. Who said anything about sitting up all night or standing in the streets? We could have seats in a stand. A stand with a cover over it —'

'Never get 'em this late,' Granny had mumbled.

Gwendoline had cried out, 'Could I see the Queen really, Daddy? Daddy, would we see the Queen in her gold carriage?'

Clagg regarded her fondly for a moment, ignoring his mother-in-law, and then said, 'Right up close enough to wave to and she'd wave straight back.' He turned to the others. 'That's how it would be. There was an article in the paper this morning how you could get tickets. We could manage it —'

'Hmpf!' Granny had snorted. 'If what? I read the article myself. Ten pounds apiece. That's for millionaires.'

'If,' Will concluded, 'we went without our summer hols.'

This, for an instant, stilled the clamour within their breasts as well as their excited outcries. Their annual two weeks' holiday at Morecambe Bay was something wonderful and treasured, and was looked forward to by each of them.

To begin with, Clagg's status and salary as foreman

made it possible. For Violet Clagg it meant two precious weeks of boarding out, eating food cooked by someone else from dishes washed by another, walking on floors scrubbed by a person paid to do it and sleeping in beds she hadn't had to make.

For Granny it provided whole new sets of ears into which to pour her views on the decadence of everything, the awfulness of modern times and the uselessness of the present generation. And to the children it promised two weeks of heaven: paddling, puddling, swimming, splashing, digging and shrimping, plus all the marvellous and unfamiliar sights and sounds and smells and foods of the seaside. The beach and pier with its games and booths, shops and donkey rides, were paradise itself. Things were there to be bought and tried or tasted with pocket money which their father allowed them for their holiday and which were, of course, never encountered in Little Pudney. Rain or shine made no difference to the boat rides or the band concerts, or for that matter to anything. Christmas and birthdays were secondary festivals. Weeks were counted from 29 August, when they packed up and went home, until the next glorious and seemingly never-arriving 15 August, when once more they would pile into the family car at Little Pudney, Morecambe-bound.

'That's it,' Clagg threw into the stunned silence. 'I've worked it out. We can't do both. We'd all have to make a sacrifice. Which do you want?' And then unable to resist the temptation to turn the scales just a trifle in the direction of his own desires, he added, 'It isn't often there's a Coronation, is it – and a Queen?'

The magic of the word 'Queen' ran through all of them, even stirring old Granny a little, for she remembered Queen Victoria in her last years.

Yet Clagg had no need to coax the rest of his family on to his side, for the Coronation fever was burning in them and had been for weeks. Already they had put up decorations in the living-room – red, white and blue paper ribbon from the four corners to the chandelier and thence to the fireplace over which hung a picture of the Queen. They had expected on the day the Queen was crowned they would take some part in the celebrations that were being planned in Little Pudney. Now suddenly, unexpectedly and stirringly, the head of the family proposed to move them to the very centre of things, and to Gwendoline Clagg this meant seeing with her own eyes, the adored figure of the Queen.

'Daddy, Daddy, I want to see the Queen!' She had not even thought or reflected over the choice. She didn't know what she expected from this transformation of the nightly going-to-sleep dream into the reality of a person, she only knew that she yearned for it. She would look upon the face of the Queen, her eyes, her hair, and her golden crown.

If Gwendoline craved to see her fantasies thus turned into reality, it was quite the opposite with her brother, who was prone to abandon this same reality for the glory of dreams. Johnny Clagg, aged eleven, was outwardly a most ordinary little boy. He was ordinary in size and looks, at his studies, at kicking a football or bowling at stumps, but the achievements of the John Clagg who lived within this undistinguished person were limitless and magnificent.

They were mostly of a military nature. He had already left Sherwood Forest behind him; he was done with knights in armour. World War II and its soldiers, which was in full tide when he had been born, had captured his lively imagination. His consuming obsession was the Army, and his recurring daydream was winning promotion from Private to Captain Clagg on the field of battle. He was Rifleman, Grenadier, Sapper, Engineer, Dispatch Rider, Tank Commander, Artilleryman, indestructible and heroic. Backing these dreams were picture-books and coloured cards of soldiers and their implements. In his toy cupboard were lead troops and a miniature tank, jeep and field-piece to deploy on the living-room floor. But outside the occasional uniformed soldier home on leave and an obsolete World War I cannon mounted in the main square of Great Pudney, Johnny had never seen the real thing. Now the glorious glittering pageant of the military might of Great Britain and the Commonwealth was offered to be paraded before his eyes. The two weeks by the sea faded into insignificance.

For Violet Clagg the dilemma was more severe. The two weeks were her rest and her recovery, to be weighed against the thrill, glamour and excitement of being in London on that day. It was she, more than any of them, who knew how right her husband had been when he used the word 'sacrifice'. And then in her mind she made it, not for herself so much as for the children. When Johnny and Gwendoline grew up they would be able to say that they had been to London for the Coronation of the Queen.

'Well, what do you say?' Clagg had queried them. 'It's one or t'other. We'll put it to a vote. All in favour of going to the Coronation say "Aye"!'

The treble voices of Johnny and Gwendoline fairly screamed out their 'Ayes'. Violet's voice was heard too.

'All those against?'

'It's a squandering of money I call it,' said Granny. 'The children need the sunshine and the sea air.' It was not so much that she didn't want to go as that she found it constitutionally impossible to agree with anything that any of the others wanted.

Will Clagg, who was usually infuriated by Granny's intransigence, now did something unusual for him. He went over and chucked the old lady under the chin. 'Come on, Granny,' he said, 'you were around when the last Queen was buried, weren't you? Don't you want to see the new one crowned? I'm voting "Aye".'

Granny Bonner found herself so powerfully and astonishingly moved that she had to blink her eyes lest the others see. It was true, she was the living link between two Queens of England. 'Well,' she equivocated, 'I suppose it mightn't hurt for one summer if we stay at home.'

'That makes it unanimous,' Will Clagg had said. The

children had begun to scream and clap their hands and jump about.

*

All day long the registered letter from London, sender Albert Capes, 3 Clacton Road, S.W.14. had been sitting upon the mantelpiece intriguing and tantalising Violet, and Granny as well, though she wouldn't have admitted it. It had arrived, of course, after Clagg had departed for the mill and the children to school and there was no doubt that it contained the tickets for the Coronation, for the week before Clagg had posted off the money order to his cousin with instructions to purchase them. There they were then surely, in the brown manila cover, thick, bulky, heavier than any letter they had ever received before. There, in that pregnant envelope, reposed the equivalent of those fourteen blissful days at the Shore View Hotel, just outside Morecambe proper.

It was, of course, unthinkable that Vi would open an envelope addressed to her husband, but she found it difficult not to break the seal. For she wanted something to hold, to see and feel, something material which might perhaps begin to alleviate the pangs of the lost holiday. The lure and the excitement of the Coronation were un-diminished, but it was as yet too abstract for her to grasp. Those lazy, restful days at the summer hotel, where she

18

didn't have to appear in the dining-room for a cooked breakfast until half past eight if she didn't wish to, were something tangible and experienced. The same holiday spent at home in Little Pudney would be just like every other week except that Will would be there cluttering up the house, making Granny even more irritable, while the children would be about with nothing to do.

Granny, too, had been having second thoughts on the validity of giving up all of the pleasant features lumped under the one heading of 'change of air' for one day of excitement which probably included being trampled underfoot or getting lost. Each time she passed the envelope on the mantelpiece she would mutter something to herself which Violet could not quite catch, but by the tone of her voice and her mother's more than usually sour expression she knew that it was disapproving. It seemed as though the day would never draw to a close.

Yet at last evening had come, bringing the accustomed heavy footfalls on the pavement approaching the house.

Granny said, 'Late, isn't he?'

Violet glanced at the clock. 'He'll have stopped for one at the George and Dragon." The children at their home-work heard him and came rushing into the front room, shouting, 'It's Dad! Will he open it? Can we see them now?' And then as he made his entrance, 'Dad, they've come, they've come! Open it!'

This Will Clagg had done, after a suitable moment's pause to assert dignity and authority and examine the exterior of the registered envelope to his satisfaction.

With the children watching impatiently and even Granny looking over her spectacles and stretching her neck from her corner, he had slit the envelope and withdrawn the wonderful, miraculous and wholly unexpected blue and gold tickets which he had now been showing around so proudly in the compartment of the Coronation Special.

At first there had been some moments of confusion as they had gaped at the pasteboards, their twenty-five guinea price mark, the location and the things promised thereon. It seemed that there must have been a mistake of some kind until Clagg noticed that in addition to the five tickets the envelope contained a letter from Bert, which he now unfolded and read aloud:

'Dear Cousin Will, here are your tickets. They are not where you wrote, they are better than where you thought because I have had a bit of luck which I am glad to pass along to you. One of the fellows in our company here has a friend who knew someone who works in the same place as a man who has the inside on what was going on with the tickets for the Coronation he said. They are marked down and I could get them because the company selling them was over-stocked and I suppose 25 guineas even here in London is pretty high and they wanted to sell them. Anyway I have got them for you for the fifty quid which is what you wanted to pay like you wrote only if it rains you will be sitting in a window drinking champagne like a toff and letting the world go by. Good luck. I wish I was with you. Sorry you are going back the same day I'd have liked to see the kiddies, give them and Vi my love. Yours Bert.'

Now all was clear at last and the wonder and the glory of it fairly dazzled them. Seats in a window! Row A! Hyde Park Corner! (The location was later checked on a map of the procession route printed in the newspapers and found to be absolutely marvellous.) Breakfast! Buffet lunch! Champagne!!!

'Champagne,' Violet Clagg whispered to herself and then repeated it out loud: 'Champagne! I've never tasted bubbly.' And in that moment the two weeks, the very necessary, needed and longed-for two weeks at the Shore View Hotel were wiped from her mind as if a sponge had passed across a chalked slate. It was replaced immediately by a new picture, one plagiarised from scenes from a number of films: the uniformed, dignified-looking butler in the drawing-room holding the napkin-wrapped bottle: 'More champagne, m'lady?' Only this time the person holding the thin-stemmed glass waiting for the froth of the high-priced wine to gush into it was not the Countess of Kissmefoot, but Violet Clagg sitting in Row A of the window in Wellington Crescent, Hyde Park Corner. As the Queen went by she would be sipping her first glass of champagne. The years had fallen away from her and suddenly she was like her own children. She had found that bright bit of something that attracts and sells, and every feminine fibre of her was reaching for it.

Even Granny was impressed and found the excitement infectious, though she would have preferred gin to champagne. She had to get in her nasty remark, of course, saying, 'If I know Bert the seats will be behind a pillar, or Row A will be the last row instead of the first.' Yet she grudgingly admitted that with breakfast and lunch being served they would not have to take along any sandwiches or fruit for the children and that would save a lot of bother.

And so all of them were gathered there now in the compartment of the Coronation Special, the Clagg family basking in the admiration of their fellow travellers, each one cherishing the particular fancy or dream to which the blue and gold tickets would admit them. The wheels sang their dickety-clax, dickety-clax, and with each turn brought them all closer to the manner in which they were to realise them.

*

Promptly at seven o'clock that morning the engine of the Coronation Special snaked its way into St Pancras Station, where it came to a halt, sighing steam and panting as though out of breath from the trip's exertions. London that morning was enveloped in a chill, grey drizzle, though the real and memorable Coronation Day downpour had not yet commenced in earnest. A bitter wind whipped the flags and bunting on the buildings and set the gay banners strung across the streets dancing an early-morning tarantella.

The Clagg family emerging from the station kept close together, for never before had they found themselves in such a welter of hurrying humanity, cars, taxis and buses.

Further greeting their astonished and excited eyes were the scrawled placards of the news-vendors: 'Queen's Day! Everest conquered! Hillary reaches Top.'

'What's Everest, Dad?' Johnny Clagg asked. Anything conquered was in his domain.

'A mountain,' replied his father. 'The highest mountain in the world. Someone has climbed it,' and bought a paper.

Johnny's interest cooled at once. Mountains and mountain-climbing were not his dish unless one took them by storm in the face of devastating enemy fire. But Will Clagg, dipping into the front-page news, felt the thrill of pride and an oddly kindred feeling for a man named Hillary who had accomplished the feat with such pat and extraordinary timing. Obviously he had made a do-or-die effort for his Queen to present her with this hitherto unclimbed peak as a gift for her Coronation Day. Well, he, Will Clagg, could climb no mountains, but he could bring his family to London for her. And there they all were.

He had the simple good sense to ask a policeman about buses and produced the tickets, which the constable

23

examined with respect and admiration. It seemed, according to the officer, that there was no problem at all; a No. 73 bus, that one right over there, would take them all the way, travelling down Tottenham Court Road into Oxford Street and thence down Park Lane and round Hyde Park Corner. He was not sure whether the buses would still be running through that area, but they should not have too far to walk and at any rate there would be plenty of police to direct them to their proper destination.

In spite of the drizzle and the damp, their first glimpse of London that early morning fulfilled every expectation. As they bowled down Oxford Street there were 'Ohs' and 'Ahs' and 'Look there!' an 'Oh, Daddy, see that?' or 'Oh, Mummy, isn't it beautiful?' when they passed beneath triumphal archways in gold and blue, topped with the Royal Arms, or rode by shop fronts draped from top to bottom with red, white and blue bunting with colourful pennants and streamers or decked out with rich, armorial banners.

Selfridge's alone was worth coming far to see, emblazoned and bedecked with flags and heraldry. The streets packed with crowds were a sight in themselves, and as they proceeded down Park Lane their bus sometimes was blocked by the swarms of people endlessly streaming in the direction of Hyde Park Corner before the barrier gates were shut. When the bus was stopped the whispering susurration and shuffling of their feet could be heard, for inner London was a silent city that day.

The vehicle on which they were travelling managed to be one of the last permitted near the area of Wellington Place, and halted at St George's Hospital on the corner of Knightsbridge. The bus conductor, who had been alerted to the destination of the Clagg family, tapped Will on the shoulder and said, 'Your stop, sir. Go straight along down past the 'orspital if you can make your way, and you'll come to Wellington Crescent.' And he added, 'You ought to have a good view.'

They dismounted and were engulfed at once in a tumultuous ocean of humanity, and Clagg understood what the bus conductor had meant by saying, 'If you can make your way.' For here were thousands upon thousands of people pushing, shoving, thronging, rubbing shoulders through the area of the great square, some trying to reach the stands, others attempting to get closer to the front ranks already packed solid along the route of procession, roped off and kept clear by the police. Everyone was in the grip of Coronation fever and the very density of the packed crowd and its gaiety made it the most thrilling experience the Claggs had ever known. This was what they had come for and they were now a part of it.

But even more enthralling as they tried, at times almost in vain, to press their way through the throngs in the direction indicated by the bus conductor, was the magic worked by the tickets they possessed, which Will Clagg now held in his hand as he led the way.

'Tickets? This way, sir! Wellington Crescent? Down

there, sir. Open up, please, and let these people through. They're ticket-holders.'

There were police lines within police lines and lanes roped off and forbidden areas, and others marked 'Ticket-holders only', and the talisman pasteboards clutched by Clagg melted them through every barrier, visible and invisible. Never before in their lives had any of them been 'special' or deferred to in anything. When there were queues, they queued; when there were 'Keep Out' signs, they kept out. And here they were among the favoured. It was heady wine which gave them all the sweetest sensation and made Will Clagg a most proud and happy man.

'Tickets, sir?' said another constable. 'Let's have a look at them. Wellington Crescent, that's just below there, sir. First on your right. Come round this way, you'll find it easier going.'

He led them round the corner of a huge wooden-grandstand slanting row upon row to the sky, the front covered with red, white and blue bunting already limp and soaked. Many people were sitting on the narrow wooden planks under blankets or with newspapers over their heads, huddled against the chilly rain.

Will Clagg experienced an even greater satisfaction. 'There, see,' he pointed out, 'that might be us if it weren't for Cousin Bert. Out in the wet and cold. In a minute we'll all be dry and snug.'

They marched along the rows of stands and for once

Granny had nothing unpleasant to contribute. She, too, had succumbed to the flattery of the treatment they had been receiving as well as to the contagion of mounting excitement from the crowds, the flags and the spirit of festival.

Thus afforded a short cut, they moved along more rapidly until they reached the far side of the square, where once more they found themselves bucking a human tide flowing in the other direction, and again friendly and helpful constables eased their way through until Clagg, looking up at a street-sign posted on the corner house, raised his arm and shouted to them, 'There! There it is!' The sign read: 'Wellington Crescent, S.W.1' to match the address on the wonderful tickets.

The Crescent was just what its name implied, a scimitar of a street sweeping up from Wellington Square towards Belgravia, and because of its shape the first dozen or so houses had a view of the traffic circle, or a part of it; though, of course, as one moved further west the angle increased and the area of view diminished.

'Come along then!' Will Clagg cried, herding and hustling his brood in front of him, noting with satisfaction that the corner house of the Crescent was No. 1, that in its windows on the first and second floors were arranged seats of planking where people were sitting or standing about with their coats off, and some of them appeared to be eating and drinking. 'Let's get in out of the wet. We could all do with a bit of breakfast, couldn't we?'

They passed Nos. 2 and 3. People holding tickets that appeared to be similar to theirs were passing in through the front doors. In a first-floor window was a whole row of children in party dress, their faces shining with excitement, each clutching either a small pennant or a stick on which were fastened red, white and blue streamers, which they waved even though there was nothing to wave at. Behind them a maid was pouring something and another passing buns. This was exactly as described, word for word, on their own admissions. Clagg's stomach could already feel the warmth and comfort of the hot tea descending.

Clagg now quickly turned to look towards the great open plaza whence they had come. The angle and the view were still perfect, and thus he didn't quite take in the fact that after No. 3 there occurred a gap in the buildings, crossed by heavy black beams stretching from the wall of No. 3 to where they supported that of the next house. But when he reached this further house and looked up to see, its number was not 4 but 6. And beyond 6 were Nos. 7, 8 and 9, still affording a view. 10 and 11 were beyond the angle. The windows were shuttered. Since they could not see they appeared to have closed their eyes.

'Wait,' Will said, 'We must have passed it. Stay here.' He retraced his steps quickly and counted again to make certain. 1, 2, 3, and then only that gaping space crossed by beams of timber; no numbers 4 or 5.

The wind, perishingly cold, seemed to have increased;

the rain as well; the outside of his mack was wet and now suddenly Will Clagg found himself damp within as well, as perspiration began to ooze from his arm-pits. He quickly counted again, and then, in alarm and half in relief at having been such a fool, he rushed to the other side of the street. But there were no houses there at all, only the long stretch of set-back buildings of the hospital biting deeply into the Crescent. He returned whence he had come, running almost blindly past his family in the grip of panic.

A police constable was standing on the pavement talking with two thick-set men in the drab, unmistakable garb that proclaimed them plain-clothes detectives. Will stepped up to the policeman. 'Beg your pardon, but could you tell me where No. 4 might be, Officer?'

The constable eyed him gravely; his two companions stirred inside their mackintoshes and moved just that fraction of an inch nearer.

Fear came to Clagg in a sickening wave. There was something familiar in these attitudes. He had seen groups such as these on street corners in Little Pudney, and had observed just such grave concentration as some shady-looking stranger had passed by.

'Now why would you be wanting No. 4?' asked the constable.

Clagg produced his blue and gold embossed tickets, and suddenly the feel of them was no longer a comfort to him as they had been from the time he had first possessed them. Now, as he held them in his fingers, it was as though, quite suddenly, they had been drained of all their beauty and virtue.

One of the men in plain clothes said, 'Here's another.' His eyes travelled to the group surrounding Will – the wife, the children, the obvious grandmother – and he added, half under his breath, 'And the family too, that's rotten!' The two men came closer to inspect the tickets.

'Well, now,' the P.C. said gently, 'if there was a No. 4 it would be here. But as you see –'

As they could all see indeed! They turned to follow the line of the constable's look and saw what he saw, and what they had seen before, and what no amount of looking or staring or fearing or wishing or hoping could change. There was no house there at all, only a gap in which grew the ubiquitous fireweed where once had stood the bombed and burned out Nos. 4 and 5.

Mrs. Clagg did not yet understand and her gaze wandered, uncomprehending, from the policeman to the empty space, to her husband's face which had now gone quite white with an alarm that could no longer be conquered. Granny Bonner's mouth was falling into a grim line and the wrinkles crossing her brow doubled. There was no doubt in *her* mind as to what was afoot. In the thickening atmosphere of apprehension the children began to look anxiously into the faces of their elders.

The second plain-clothes detective asked, 'Can you tell us who sold you these tickets?'

In one sickening, heart-breaking moment the heretofore

good, decent, honest British universe was collapsing about Clagg. And standing there among the shards it came to him that he must face the fact that his cousin Bert was either a crook himself or the biggest fool in the world. Neither of these contingencies was to be admitted before a stranger. 'No,' he replied.

Granny's eyes glowered behind her spectacles. Her arms went akimbo in the gesture that Clagg knew all too well; she was going to make a speech. 'If it was me,' she snapped, 'I'd tell 'em. I have a good mind to right now –'

'Be quiet!' ordered Will, and the menace that flamed suddenly into his heavy, anguished face frightened and silenced her. 'It wasn't his fault. He thought he was doing us proud. It could happen to anyone.'

Now, for the first time, the full import of the catastrophe was brought home to Violet Clagg, who translated the empty space where the house should have been into her own terms of disaster. 'Then there won't be any bubbly!' she wailed. For at that moment this was as far as she could see and tears commenced to fall from her eyes. Frightened, Gwenny began to cry too without knowing why.

Johnny asked, 'Dad, what's happened? What's wrong, Dad?'

Will Clagg replied bitterly, 'We've been swindled!'

The wind sighed around the curve of the Crescent and blew bitingly from the gaping hole. Behind its chilly front the light drizzle turned into heavy rain. Granny reached for the children, tugging their raincoats tighter about them

31

and buttoning up their collars with the harsh, jerky move-
ments employed by grown-ups with their young when
they are irritated. 'If I ever lay my hands on that Bert –'
she muttered, yanking at the buttonhole of Johnny's
collar so that the boy said, 'Ow, Granny!' and stiffened
in resistance.

The first detective pounced upon the name. 'Bert, eh?
Bert who?'

Will turned on Granny savagely. 'I told you to keep
your bloody mouth shut!' Then to the detective, 'Bert
nobody! I bought 'em from a fellow in the street outside
St Pancras.'

And there they were, the two groups with a wall
between them – the constable, the two suspicious detectives and the innocent Claggs, with the latter somehow
forced into the position of being not *quite* that innocent.
They had something to hide. Clagg had nothing against
the police and always got on well with the men on post
back home, yet he was of that environment to whom a
copper was a copper and never wholly to be trusted.

Violet Clagg said weakly, 'But look at the name of the
comp'ny on the tickets where it says No. 18 Victoria Road.
Maybe we could go there and get our money back.'

The second detective said wearily, 'Ma'am, we've been
there already. That's another hole in the ground. So far
it's been mostly Americans and Australians that's got stuck
with these.' He snorted. 'Description of man selling same –
two eyes, ears, a nose and a mouth. But if you could help

32

us with this 'ere Bert we might have a chance to collar one or two of those spivs—'

Clagg snatched the tickets back from the detective who was holding them and asked angrily, 'Would it get us what's called for – a view of the procession, breakfast and that there buffet lunch with champagne?'

'No,' replied the detective, 'but—'

'Then there wasn't any Bert,' Clagg said curtly. 'Come to think of it, it was more like Joe or Sam.'

The two detectives and the policeman stood regarding him heavily at this obviously mendacious statement. They made a kind of static islet in the constantly moving stream of people. Here were more Londoners come from all quarters of the vast city, visitors from out of town, vendors of programmes, flags, balloons and souvenirs, all swarming in one direction. The rain poured down upon them and they simply ignored it. For them it didn't exist. Nothing could dampen their enthusiasm or extinguish their gaiety of spirit, their pride in being British and their joy in being alive that day. The area was full of the sounds of the eternal shuffling of feet, of laughter and chatter, shouts and cries, and one heard the word 'Everest' a great deal. Every so often parties holding valid and proper tickets detached themselves from the stream and entered into valid, proper and existing houses where genuine seats were built behind *bona fide* transparent windows and where no doubt breakfast, lunch and champagne *would* be served.

It was obvious to Clagg that there was nothing more

to be gained by remaining there. He gathered up his family with a gesture. 'Come along, let's get out of here.'

A gust of wind bounced drops of rain off the helmet of the policeman and ballooned the tan mackintoshes of the two detectives. One of them said, 'Just a moment, sir. We'd better have those tickets,' and reached out his hand. From somewhere inside himself the constable produced a note-book and pencil stub, which he shielded from the rain with a cupped hand. 'I'll have to have your name and address, sir.'

Clagg turned upon them angrily. 'What the devil for? I've paid for them! All right, so I've got stuck. Can't you leave us be? We've 'ad it! We're making no complaint.'

The detective said, 'Evidence, sir. You want those fellows laid by the heels, don't you? That's a cruel hoax they've worked. Look at you and your family—'

Johnny Clagg wailed, 'I wanted to keep mine as a souvenir.'

The detective's hand was still outstretched for them. There was nothing for Clagg to do but give them over. The man inspected them gravely, nodding his head. His partner said, not unkindly, to Johnny, 'When we've done with them we'll send 'em back to you, if you like. They might just help us to catch those twisters now, mightn't they?'

The constable poised his pencil again. 'Your name please, sir?'

In his anger it was on the tip of Will Clagg's tongue to reply, 'John Smith,' but he suddenly found his wrath shifting not only to the swine who had perpetrated this filthy trick, but to his cousin Bert as well. Was there not some kind of a law against giving a false name and address to the police? From being an innocent victim of a rotten swindle he was finding himself manoeuvred on to the side of the crooks, not only defending them but on the verge of himself becoming an accomplice by giving a wrong name and address. 'Will Clagg,' he replied, 'No. 56 Imperial Road, Little Pudney.'

'Occupation?'

'Foreman, No. 2 Rolling Mill, Pudney Steel Works.'

The constable's eyes rested upon Clagg's form for an instant in an appraisal that Clagg felt was not unadmiring. In that glance the constable had acknowledged him as a person of worth and importance, and Clagg experienced a moment of warmth for and understanding of the police-man engaged in his duty.

'Wife's name?'

'Violet Clagg.'

'Wife's mother or yours?'

'Wife's. Elsie Bonner.'

'Kids?'

'John J. and Gwendoline R.'

'There now,' said the policeman having finished his writing, 'you wouldn't want to change your mind about that there Bert, would you?'

For a moment Clagg was tempted. If the crooks *might* be traced through his cousin . . . Then his loyalty asserted itself again. 'No!'

The constable nodded as though he understood and said, 'If we ever turn those fellows up, you'll be notified.'

Clagg merely said, 'Come on,' again to his family and they began to move off. The two detectives watched them go with sad, too-wise eyes.

*

The three grown-ups, and in particular Will Clagg, were too numbed for the moment by the disaster to know what they were doing or which way they were going. It was bad luck, therefore, that instead of heading for Wellington Place, where the barriers were still open, they moved, stunned and defeated, in the opposite direction towards Belgrave Square.

Gwenny was not only too young to understand what had happened, but likewise too absorbed in the anticipation of seeing the Queen in her golden carriage. But Johnny, who was older and wiser, had a moment of panic communicated to him by the behaviour of the grown-ups. He was aware that there was something very wrong with the tickets they had bought and he had never seen the great god who was his father so flustered or put out. Yet not that easily was this figure demolished. Dad always somehow managed to set right things that had gone wrong and would undoubtedly do so again. In the meantime here he was for for the first time in his life plunged into the excitement that was London on Coronation Day. Somewhere the soldiers he had come to see would be forming up for the grand processional parade and sooner or later he was bound to encounter them. His faith in his father remained undiminished.

Not so Granny, whose tongue had not stopped clacking from the moment they had got out of earshot of the detectives. The rise and fall of her querulous voice ran on and on like some incongruous background commentary on the wireless, on the gullibility of men, but in particular the stupidity of Bert and Will.

'Oh do be quiet, Mum,' Violet said suddenly and sharply, and to her own great surprise. 'It wasn't Will's fault or Bert's either. They both wanted us to have the best there was.' She was startled at her own temerity at speaking up thus to her mother, but the feeling of her husband's pain and humiliation had communicated itself to her and touched her and she had spoken before she was aware of it.

'Humph,' said Granny, 'you've got to stick up for him, of course. You know as well as I do that I'm right.' But she subsided then and walked along through the cold, steady rain, her lips moving silently, her gimlet eyes hard and angry.

Will Clagg's preoccupation as they retreated from the

scene of their defeat was not so much who was to blame or the extent of his responsibility for what had happened and was happening; it was his world which had been shattered. Over and above his concern for the disappointment his children were about to suffer was the realisation of the penetration of his safe, homely British world by something evil, crooked and destructive.

An honest day's work for an honest day's pay was what Will Clagg had always delivered and received. He lived in simplicity and decency under a reasonably secure system. True, there were police and there were thieves and murderers, yes, and tricksters too on a grand scale, and the newspapers were always entertainingly full of robberies and bashings, rapine and murder, kidnapping and arson, gigantic swindles and the mulctings of widows and orphans. But all these things always happened to someone else. Never before had any crime been directed at him, since he had never owned anything worth stealing. For the first time, then, he had been compelled to acknowledge the savage jungle surrounding him. Curiously enough, his usually stolid mind provided a sudden moment of imaginative creation in which he saw the counterfeiters in their den bending over their engraving tools and stamping machines, grinning and sniggering as they mocked up the tickets with which to cheat Will Clagg and his family.

Clagg had suffered a blow. He was aware that neither he nor life thereafter would ever be quite the same again.

He had learned a crushing lesson with regard to bargains, but it was his family who would most truly suffer from it and it was this that angered him almost to the point of tears. He was so completely helpless. The crooks would never be turned up. And what if they were? The Coronation with all the joys and excitement they would miss would long be over.

In the meantime he marched on blindly and dumbly, and his family followed him, none of them knowing whither they were going. Thus they passed from Belgrave Square up William Street into Knightsbridge, where again they encountered crowds streaming eastwards.

They stood there under the grey weeping skies for a moment, watching the people. From the direction of the river, borne on the rain-laden gusts of wind, came a distant thudding. Johnny Clagg pricked up his ears. 'Guns!' he cried excitedly.

The sound of the saluting cannon seemed to point up all they were being denied. For an instant Will Clagg caved in completely, sick at heart and defeated. 'All right,' he said, 'we've had it. I'm a fool. I've queered it. We'd better go home.'

Violet Clagg took his arm. 'Don't take it so to heart, Will. It wasn't your fault.' The word 'home' penetrated to both children and they sent up an anguished wail of protest, but oddly enough it was Granny now who put her foot down.

'Go home?' she repeated. 'And disappoint the children?

Nonsense! I came here to see the Coronation and that's what I'm going to see. We're as damp as we can be now. We can stand.'

They all stared at her in astonishment and none more startled than her son-in-law. Granny somehow looked a little less grim and forbidding. A small measure of the dignity of refusal to be defeated by adverse fates had come into her small grey figure.

'Well, I'm blowed,' said Clagg. 'Do you mean that, Granny?'

'Mean it? Of course I do, and don't stand there talking and wasting time, Will Clagg, when we ought to be going along to find some place where these poor children can see *something*.'

'Well, I'm blowed,' Clagg repeated, and then his spirits suddenly lifted. 'Good for you, old girl. Who would have thought it? What do you vote, Vi?'

'If you don't think the children will get too wet.'

'They're wet as they can get now, but dry enough inside, I'll wager. What's a little bit of rain, eh? Come on then, off we go.' He took his daughter's small hand in his huge thick paw and said, 'You're going to see the Queen just like I promised you.'

There was no problem as to which direction they should take. They were like punters pulled up at the side of a fast-moving stream; they had only to push themselves out into the current to be carried along. And on they went now, hopeful, cheered and united again, prepared to put the best face possible on the matter and save what was left of the day.

Suddenly, however, they found their progress slowing as those in front of them came almost to a halt; others continued pushing, threatening to compress them.

Then from ahead there arose a shout from the crowd, which turned into a great roar of protest, and, standing for a moment on tiptoes to enable him to look over their heads, Will Clagg saw to his horror what was happening and what had aroused the outcry.

Some fifty yards beyond where they were, police had linked arms to form a living wall behind which, for a moment, they contained the surging crowd, and into the space thus won at the back of them a solid wooden barrier, seven feet high, was being swung across the road from each side on hinges to meet in the centre, where it was locked and barred into place, as immovable as the wall that Hadrian had built against the Picts and Scots. These barriers had been erected across the streets and avenues at key points leading into the procession route around the entire perimeter of the area, enabling the police completely to seal off the Coronation district when, in their judgment, it was no longer safe to permit further crowding. They had been thrown wide early in the morning to permit buses and cars through, as well as to admit the spectators who had been streaming thither steadily since before dawn. Now the order had gone forth to bar further entrance.

Only at the centre of each was a small door, guarded by two constables within and one on the outside, to permit the passage of those who had tickets or passes, or others authorised to enter or leave the Coronation area, such as messengers, vendors, photographers, pressmen, doctors, etc.

There was no mistaking what had taken place, and, if Clagg had not been aware, the change in mood and temper of the crowd would have told him. There were cries of anger and the police came in for some plain speaking. For the second time that day Clagg felt his heart sinking helplessly in his breast. 'Oh Lord!' he cried. 'We're too late!'

'Go on,' said Granny, 'don't stop. What are you waiting for?' She was too small to see what had happened.

'There's no going on,' Will said. 'They've closed the gates. We're shut out.'

Yet there was still some movement forward, though it had turned sluggish, and the Claggs were swept along with it as those behind pushed forward, intent upon arguing with the police. They soon met the counter-thrust of those returning from the barrier with disappointment written on their faces. They were saying, 'It's no use. They won't let anybody through.'

'You tell the police what happened to us and they'll let us by,' said Granny.

Clagg was not so sure, but knew that he must try.

Ten yards away from the barrier where the policeman

was standing the struggling pack of humanity ground to a halt.

'Wait here,' Clagg said to them. 'I'll see what I can do.' And now, using his broad shoulders and powerful frame, he shoved through. The crowd, which had once seemed friendly, co-operative and hospitable, was no longer so. It took him minutes by sheer strength and drive to reach the constable at the small portal giving ingress to the barrier, and he was bathed in sweat when he arrived there.

Panting, half-blinded by rain and perspiration running into his eyes, he said, of course, quite the wrong thing for a start: 'Look here, officer, we've got to get through.'

The officer replied in a monotone like the tape recording of the time on the telephone, 'No more permitted through. Sorry, you'll have to go back. No more permitted through.'

'But I had tickets,' Clagg shouted at him.

'Tickets,' echoed the constable. 'Very well, let's have a look at them, then,' and to those who were nearest and almost on top of him he said, 'Would you mind giving way and letting this man by? He's got tickets.'

But of course Clagg had no tickets, and he now inwardly cursed himself for ever having been so stupid as to turn them over. Detective or no detective, at least he might have held out one or two.

'Well?' said the constable.

Clagg became flustered. 'I said I *had* tickets. I haven't

43

got them any more. One of your busies took them from me. They were counterfeit. Twenty-five guineas each. I brought the whole family down from Sheffield. There was nothing but a bombed-out house there,' he finished lamely.

It all sounded very fishy to the constable, who not only was young but not a Londoner. He had been imported from the West as an auxiliary to assist in the enormous job of controlling the city during the Coronation. 'What's all this,' he said, 'pushing through here saying you had tickets and then you haven't any? Acting like that won't get you anywhere.'

Two couples threaded their way through, holding up pasteboards. 'Step aside, please,' the constable said, 'and let these people by as *has* got tickets,' and his tone was heavily pointed.

In that bitter moment Clagg recrossed the awful gulf between the privileged and non-privileged. His magic talisman had been taken from him. Now that he no longer had it he was just like all the rest, to be pushed and buffeted about. As the four ticket-holders passed through, Clagg had a glimpse through the gap at the vast sea of people on the other side, or rather the backs of their heads; he could look down Piccadilly and see the trees in Green Park; then the barrier closed again.

Helpless once more in the face of the situation, Clagg could do nothing but growl, mutter and mumble and avoid looking at his family, who had now managed to join him, and then tell the story of the fraudulent seats to those nearest him. Several of them only laughed, obviously disbelieving, but some of them knew that he was telling the truth; their sense of fair play was outraged and they even shouted at the constable that it was a shame and he ought to let the Claggs through, which of course made him all the more determined to stick to his guns and his duty.

Gwendoline said suddenly, 'I'm tired, Daddy.' Clagg picked her up in his arms. She rested her head on his shoulder contentedly and trustingly, and immediately went to sleep.

They would have gone away then, and probably found their way back to St Pancras and home, or might even have managed somewhere to connect with a television set, had it not been for the inevitable rumours, one after the other, that went sweeping through the ranks of those barred from entrance, keeping hope alive.

When the first protests and attempts to pass the barrier had proved unavailing, the crowd had begun to thin and change as disappointed ones left and new ones arrived, but retained a kind of permanent core who stayed there because of bits of so-called inside information which seeped through to them: the gates would be thrown open once more within an hour; within two hours; within three. As soon as the press of people on the other side had distributed itself, more were to be permitted to enter. No, the gen was that immediately after the Crowning those that had remained outside would be allowed in.

There was no truth in any of these rumours, but they continued to multiply or gain fresh impetus whenever newcomers would arrive or at the emergence of someone from within. Every time the small door opened there would be a buzz and stir in the crowd as they caught a glimpse of the packed throng on the other side. They also saw that a space had been cleared by the police just inside the door, which furnished fuel to the hopes that they were preparing to admit them. There was even one report that when the constable guarding the portal was changed, an 'all right' chap would be coming on who would know how to close an eye and see that deserving parties managed to get inside. These quickly circulated bits of hearsay kept this knot of people standing there in the rain waiting and hoping, hour after hour through the morning. And among them were the Claggs.

They had nowhere else to go except home, defeated. As long as there seemed a chance of getting in at this point, they had to remain. And unfamiliar as they were with the manner in which false stories could circulate through a crowd, Clagg believed that here was their best opportunity rather than to go wandering about the fringe of the Coronation area in the city that was unknown to them.

And perversely enough, things *did* happen which made it appear as though they were about to win through. Such as the time when the door opened and two police sergeants, stiffly saluted by the P.C. on guard, came

46

out. They stood for a moment regarding the knot of people and conversing in low tones. Hearts began to beat in anticipation, eyes again came alight with expectancy; there were shouts of 'What about it Sergeant?' It seemed so obvious that they were looking the situation over preparatory to giving orders to have them admitted. But they only turned their backs and without even speaking to the constable returned inside again. Yet even while immediate hopes were dashed, how could one know that, having looked the situation over, they would not make their report within, after which action in favour of those waiting would be taken? At least so the grape-vine had it, and the Claggs stayed on.

Gwendoline awakened, lifted her head from her father's shoulder and asked sleepily, 'Is the Queen coming?'

He put her down with aching arms. Her mother pushed some damp locks away from her forehead and said, 'Not yet, luvvy. Have another little nap.'

Granny said, 'Why don't you tell her? She isn't ever going to see her.'

'I can't,' replied Will Clagg in agony.

For the first time Johnny Clagg became aware of the true nature of the situation. 'Aren't we going to see *anything*?' he yammered.

Clagg had to lie to him. 'Not yet. Maybe later.' He wondered whether with the little money he had on him he might bribe the policeman to let them through, and simultaneously knew that never in a million years would

47

he be able to approach the constable with such a proposition, nor in as many aeons would the man ever accept it. In the meantime the rain continued to fall and in the distance there was a pealing of bells.

And just when all euphoria occasioned by the incident of the police sergeants had been drained away, there occurred another diversion: a party of young people arrived, well bundled up against the weather, three girls and two boys just out of their teens. They had with them an umbrella, a small portable radio and a packet of sandwiches. With that extreme and happy disregard of youth for what goes on about them, they had apparently never heard of or read the long complicated rules laid down by the authorities governing pedestrian and vehicular movement on Coronation Day, and blithely demanded admission of the harassed constable. Denied it, they made no protest but, sheltering the wireless beneath the umbrella, switched it on and formed themselves into a circle to listen.

The voice of the commentator inside Westminster Abbey came through. Those standing nearby, including the Claggs, moved closer to hear and soon there was a ring of listeners gathered about the young people. They and their portable set were a centre of attraction, and this made them happy.

The contact furnished by the voice emerging from the little speaker brought the Claggs back to life again. They were filled with gratitude for it and it seemed as though things had suddenly taken a turn for the better and they listened eagerly. It didn't strike them that they might have been hearkening to the same commentary in the warmth and comfort of their own home.

'Listen to what the man is saying,' Violet Clagg admonished the two children. 'He's talking about the Queen.'

The subdued voice of the commentator from within the Abbey came through: 'In a moment you will be hearing the fanfare which will be the signal for the presentation of the Queen to the peers of the realm by the Archbishop of Canterbury—'

*

High up in the eaves of the Abbey trumpeters with one unanimous movement set their silver bannereted instruments to their lips and blew a fanfare that went echoing through the great church, shattering the silences through vault and nave. It was the signal for the Ceremony of Recognition, that exquisitely beautiful anachronism in which the queen to be crowned was made known to the nobles of her realm gathered to acknowledge her.

The Queen, attired in gold-embroidered white, was a tiny figure in a pool of light, standing on the blue-carpeted floor in the centre of the Abbey. The colour of her raiment was symbolic, for that day too she would become the bride of England, wedded indissolubly to the State, the

Church and British subjects throughout the world.

This was one of those astounding moments in the history of the taming and civilising of man in which he relinquished all his great temporal power in the face of the spiritual ideal.

There stood a lone woman, as gentle and helpless as a butterfly. She had no power beyond the history and the travail of the nation she represented. There were no armies at her back. At her side stood only a benign old man in a glittering green cope, holding a cross.

The might of man appeared to be personified by the black-clad figure of the Lord Chancellor in his great and terrifying wig, the Lord High Chamberlain, the Earl Marshal, and the Garter King of Arms in his multi-coloured tabard, seeming almost to be arrayed against her, and by the vast aggregation of men and women, peers and nobles, hemming her in on all four sides.

In the stillness that followed the drifting away of the last echoes of the fanfare to the vaulted stone of the Abbey eaves was heard the old, clear, portentous voice of the Archbishop of Canterbury, as for a moment he clasped the small, white hand of the Queen and, turning with her to all that conglomeration of shapes and faces looking towards the east, he said: 'Sirs, I here present unto you Queen Elizabeth, the undoubted Queen of this Realm; wherefore all you who are come this day to do her homage and service, are you willing to do the same?'

The shout of their reply came at once, short and sharp:

'God save Queen Elizabeth!'

Once more the fanfare from the silver trumpets pealed down from the roof, and the Queen curtsied in a most exquisite gesture to the peers assembled.

She was so very young and graceful, and the inclination of her head and body to the gentlemen was poignantly tender, yet at the same time yielding not one iota of dignity. There was contained in this movement both appeal as well as authority, and it was this appeal which was so infinitely touching, so that those who looked upon it could not keep their throats from constricting or tears from their eyes. She was asking for their recognition and acknowledgement, for without it she was no more than a frail and vulnerable human; and at the same time she demanded this acceptance by right of birth, lineage, inheritance and the concurrence of God.

For the instant, history and tradition were alive and quivering, and one expected almost a great voice like an organ peal thundering from on high: 'Do you, the people of Great Britain, take this woman, Elizabeth, for your lawful wedded Queen as long as you both shall live?'

Four times did the trumpets blare, four times did the venerable Archbishop voice his query, four times did the brown head incline as the small, proud figure swept her curtsy to the north, the south, the east and the west, to be acclaimed and accepted by the four quarters of the globe.

*

The hushed commentary from the Abbey emerging from the little wireless set beneath the umbrella suddenly turned into music and the nasal rasp of a man singing in French. There had been a dull portion of the ceremony from within the Abbey while the Queen was being garbed and one of the boys had simply switched to a station in France.

It brought back Will Clagg with a wrench to the truth of their situation, and he fell prey to a sudden onslaught of unreasoning rage at the shabby trick fate had played upon them, and during a surge of temper that welled up from within him he came close to charging the gate with his burly shoulders in an attempt to crash through it so that he might fulfil the promise he had made to his daughter that she should see the Queen.

The wave subsided. His workman's eye told him that this barrier had been built to resist the pressure of thousands. Violence would accomplish nothing. Yet what were they to do and where were they to go? All of them hoped that something might yet happen to save the day. They could not escape the feeling that by their long and patient wait there they had earned something, had in some way piled up a credit or paid some kind of fee or bribe to fate which, should they leave to try their luck elsewhere, would then be forfeit. They and the other hopefuls who had stayed were veterans of that particular sector, companions in enterprise and misery. They had made a few friends there and everyone within range knew about their mishap with the tickets and sympathised with them.

They didn't feel thus like venturing into new territory. The façade of St. George's Hospital was familiar to them, as was the Carriage Drive of Hyde Park. Every slat and board, frame and nail of the wooden barrier was known to them as well. Here they were at least a little at home.

The small door opened from the inside, causing them all to stir and rustle and move and crane their necks to look, for it was from that quarter they all hoped for their reprieve, but it was only a soaked souvenir-seller, his goods sold, his baskets all but empty, retreating to where warmth and sustenance might be found. He was a little man with bad teeth and a spiv's cunning eyes. He wore baggy clothes and his peaked cap was pulled down over his ears. He looked with some surprise at the people gathered around the barrier and then said, without much hope or animation, 'Souvenirs! Last of the lot. Who'll have one cheap?'

There was not much choice in his basket – two small dolls with red, white and blue rosettes, a sodden Union Jack on a stick, several balloons and a periscope, one of those small elongated white boxes with mirrors at each end.

'Here, wait a minute,' said Clagg. 'Let's have a look at that.'

'Just the thing, guv'ner,' the vendor said, handing over the periscope. 'Makes you eight feet tall. Look over anybody's 'ead. Fun for the kiddies afterwards. Last one, guv'ner. Five bob to you.'

Will Clagg raised the instrument and applied his eye to

the bottom. It might have worked inside to see over the heads of taller people, but here it just barely reached to the top of the barrier, giving a glimpse of the upper part of the archway and some foliage. It was hopeless, and of course when he held it higher he could no longer get his eye to it. The affair was beginning to assume the qualities of a nightmare, one of those dreams where one is always missing buses or trying to escape from danger in shoes made of lead.

Clagg handed the periscope back to the vendor, who grinned at him cheerfully, showing his broken teeth, and said, 'Bit of short measure there, guv'ner. You should have growed some more. What about something for the kiddies?'

'Shut your bloody trap! Here, let's see what you've got.' He bought a doll for Gwendoline and the wet flag for Johnny.

Violet said, 'Say thank you to Daddy,' and Gwendoline did, but her mind was elsewhere, on the Queen. She was wondering how ever she could manage to put all of her love into one smile and one wave when the moment came that she would see the Queen drive by in her golden carriage. She thought perhaps she would wave both hands at once.

As for Johnny he was old enough, and by now sufficiently wise to know that his Union Jack was not for waving, that it would never join the sea of fluttering pennons which would be set in motion on the other side of the barrier. Instead, therefore, he planted it upon the escarpment topping Hill No. 5 and with the survivors of his regiment prepared to defend it to the death. Below he could see the enemy troops massing for the assault. With no thought for his own safety, he marched back and forth along the line, pistol in hand, encouraging his force. 'Stand firm, men! We'll never surrender! Let them come, we're more than a match for them!'

Shortly after noon, a squabble broke out among the young people who owned the radio, or rather between the actual owner, who appeared to be named Lionel, and the others. Lionel was a stringy boy with sideburns who was enjoying the dance music from France and was snapping his fingers and wriggling his hips to it. The girls wanted to come back to the Coronation.

'Oh, come on, Lionel,' they kept saying, 'turn it back. We want to hear when the Queen is crowned.'

'Ah, da-da, de-di, da-da,' sang Lionel, clicked his fingers and bumped his hips.

The Claggs united in hating Lionel and rooting for the girls. They too wanted to hear the Coronation. Granny muttered, 'Humph, the young people of today!'

Clagg said, 'Young squirt! If he was mine I'd teach him something.'

'Oh, come on, Lionel. Do turn it back. It's time.'

The impasse was broken by the other boy, who simply pushed Lionel out of the way and twirled the knob of the little box, and once more the soft voice of the commentator came through, and all those close to the little circle bent closer to hear him say that the moment of crowning was at hand.

*

And far off in the Abbey the Archbishop crowned the Queen and, with the placing of the heavily-jewelled, awkwardly balanced and weighty crown on to the light brown hair of the head bent slightly forward to receive it, set off such a peal of bells and thudding of cannon-fire as to reach to the farthest ends of the earth.

This was the moment of the priest, the intermediary between God and man, the Archbishop of Canterbury, charged with the transfer of spiritual power to the temporal hand and anointing her as God's representative in her realm.

Yet, too, it was the gesture and movement of a good, kindly human, an old man of experience and understanding of the frailties of the body as well as the spirit. St. Edward's crown of gold was heavy, ungainly and cumbersome. It could hurt, pressing upon the skull and forehead.

It seemed impossible almost that so many ends could be embodied in one smooth, simple gesture compounded of fatherly solicitude and the awful symbolism of majesty. There was his care and forethought for her dignity: the crown was too large for the small head beneath it, top-heavy and precarious in its seat; it must be balanced just so that it would not slip or slide or alter its position, once placed, during the long and arduous ceremony that was to follow until it was removed.

And as he lowered the shining object on to her head, he held to it for a moment yet, as though to make sure that it was comfortable and had settled firmly and securely. One felt the sigh in the heart of the old man that such a burden of responsibility should be put upon one so young, such a fearful inheritance handed on to one so gentle and frail. He was endowing her with grandeur and simultaneously bestowing upon her endless cares.

Then with a fine and paternal flourish of both hands he released it and stepped back. The great act of the Crowning was completed.

*

The sharp crack of saluting charges fired from mobile artillery stationed in nearby Hyde Park startled them all. The shots were echoed by the distant thudding of guns from the Tower of London. Bells pealed and jangled wildly from all quarters.

Will Clagg looked at his watch. It was 12.32. The cannon and the bell-ringing and the full-throated cheers from the throngs massed on the other side of the wall drowned out the little radio. He took off his hat and let the rain fall on to his head. 'The Queen has been crowned,' he said. And for a moment it didn't matter that he was standing bareheaded behind the barrier. He felt a pride and a thrust of gladness through his heart that he was there.

Violet Clagg murmured, 'God bless her,' and dabbed at her eyes with a sopping handkerchief with which she had been wiping the moisture from her neck.

Granny Bonner sniffed and said, 'Good luck to her.'

Those gathered around the wireless set cheered too, and Johnny waved his flag. But Gwendoline cried, 'Daddy, is she coming now? Daddy, I can't see anything!'

'No, no,' Clagg soothed, 'not yet, Gwenny. There's lots of time still. We'll be there when she does.' But he didn't know how.

*

Granny Bonner's feet were beginning to hurt her in her wet shoes. Her thighs ached from standing. She was hungry. Her hair was soaked. But of all things she was wishing that it would rain even harder and that somehow before the day was done even more dreadful things would happen to them than had already occurred.

For the truth was that she was having the time of her life and expected to collect from exposure to the weather such a catalogue of ills, aches and pains as would keep the Clagg family in total subjugation to her for the next six months.

Indulging Granny's miseries was a part of the ritual of living at the Claggs. To hear her tell it, she suffered from rheumatism, arthritis, sciatica, hardening of the arteries, stiffening of the joints, inflammation of the tendons, and anything else she happened to read about in the newspaper advertisements for patent medicines. One had to ask her in the morning whether she felt better, and before going to bed at night whether she thought she was going to be able to sleep. The Claggs never questioned her right to these ills, since she was an aged person and so entitled to them.

Thus she wished for thunder, lightning and hail, Ossa piled upon Pelion, did Granny, for the sake of the delicious concessions she would wring from Will Clagg, now already reduced to a worm's level by the catastrophe that she had had the good fortune to forecast.

True, the old lady also would have liked to have had a glimpse of the Queen for the very reason that her son-in-law had pointed out: she would then have seen two of the great queens of England, one deceased, the other crowned, and remained herself the living link between them. But over and against this disappointment was balanced the perverse delight she would take in telling the story of Will's idiocy. She was aware that, had all the promises of the day been kept, and she had sat in her window-seat, or even managed to stand along the route of procession with the throng, she would only have seen what everybody else saw. And what was there to tell in that? The narration of this misadventure and of its undoubted consequence would take hours to unfold and would last her as a tea-time topic to her cronies at Morecambe and Little Pudney to her dying day.

In the meantime, with no objections from either Will Clagg or Violet, who was suffering from the collapse of her husband's ego as well as everything else, Granny had elected herself captain of the children. She was bossing them unmercifully, yanking at their clothes, pulling them about one moment, commiserating with them the next, fondling and spoiling them with loud and pointed remarks about poor babes brought upon such an expedition, and doling out the small ration of chocolate she had brought along and which was all they had to quiet their hunger.

The wireless was still their link with the solemn ceremony continuing in the Abbey, and Lionel, succumbing to the will of the majority, was content to leave the instrument tuned to the B.B.C., and in fact was now basking in the attention of all those crowded around trying to hear and in the reflected glory of owning the set. From the expression on his face one might have thought that he had invented radio communication.

Thus they heard from that great church to which the voice of the commentator transported them momentarily, how the peers of the realm came and knelt at the feet of the woman who a few minutes before had undergone the mystical change that made her for ever a person apart from them all.

Not only did they kneel, but they performed a gesture symbolic of submission. They folded their hands in an attitude of prayer and placed them between hers, and by so doing bound themselves to her in loyalty everlasting.

Led by the Archbishop of Canterbury, followed then by her own husband and the father of her children, Prince Philip, great names remembered from centuries of history bent the knee before her, grey heads bowed and paid their homage. Empty and archaic the ceremony might have seemed in this day and age, but there was still an exquisite and throat-catching beauty connected with it.

But the procession of peers entitled thus to swear their fealty seemed endless as the lesser ones took their turn, and Lionel said, 'Ah, it just goes on like that. Come on, let's go.' This time he found acquiescence among his friends. He turned the dial again. Debussy emerged from the box and to his dissonants the five of them all moved off, to the regret of those remaining, for with them went their one contact with the Coronation.

What chocolate the Claggs had with them had been consumed by the children. There was no sign of any change in the order of the day or of the gates being opened to admit them. Standing there had become a habit. No one had the initiative to leave for fear they might miss something, and when inevitably the children made known their need to go to the lavatory, the Claggs proceeded to do so in relays. Fortunately they were in reach of the underground public convenience at Hyde Park Corner. Violet went first with Granny and Gwenny. Then Will trailed thither with Johnny. When they returned, somewhat refreshed, they simply continued to stand. It was as though they were all under some kind of spell which fixed them into eternity to that spot.

Will Clagg, it is true, made a half-hearted attempt to break out of the cocoon of inertia that surrounded them, but he was too beaten morally to make a job of it. He mumbled something to the effect that maybe they had all best go home and get into something warm and dry. No one answered him. To Violet home was the end of the adventure, such as it was, and, as for Granny, the day of suffering was only half over. There were still four or five hours of discomfort and misery to be banked for the future. She was in no hurry to call it off.

There was no way of knowing whether Clagg would have pursued the subject in spite of being ignored, for at that moment – and it was then shortly after two o'clock – came the sound of the *thump-thump-thump* of distant drums and the wind-wafted *oompah* of the military brasses. The procession was on its way.

The effect was immediate, electric and revivifying upon all those caught behind the barrier. The martial music stiffened their backs and brought new life into eyes dulled with fatigue and weariness. They began to chivvy the constable. 'Come on now. Are you going to let us through or not?'

The young policeman, himself moved by the distant

62

sounds, grinned uncomfortably. It felt as though something ought to be happening, yet the situation had not changed. 'I got no orders to do so,' he reiterated. 'I can't see no more myself than you can.'

'You're pyed to stand there. What abaht those kiddies come all the way from Sheffield to see the Queen?'

The constable turned his back. Nearer and nearer approached the first of the bands, thumping, shrilling and blaring forth a blood-stirring military air. The music waxed in brazen volume as the marchers emerged from the canyon of Piccadilly and burst into the square, turning the corner with the squealing of fifes, braying of brasses and the solid beating of wet drum-skins. 'Boom, boom, boompety-boom' went the rhythms and in one's mind's eye one could picture the proud drummers in their leopard aprons twirling their sticks over their heads before they brought them down to crash once more into the sides of their instruments. 'Tee-boom, tee-boom, tee-boom!' Cymbals crashed, shivered and shimmered, shaking the air with their vibrations.

To the thrilling swing of the music was now added the endless *throp-throp-throp-throp* of marching feet and the mournful, high-pitched, long-drawn-out cries of command from the officers to right wheel as they turned around the triangle past Hyde Park Corner, divided and passed through the arches leading to the East Carriage Drive.

From then on, none of those remaining behind the

barrier thought any more of leaving. The sound filled their ears, heated the blood in their veins and shook their bones. It was tantalising to the point of madness, but there was no escape from it. Without realising it, they were settling for half the loaf. If they could not see, at least they could hear. Several of those near the Claggs close to the little door were jigging up and down in time to the music. It warmed them and pleased them. In a way it was like listening to the radio as band followed band, and if there were not the tread of marchers then there would be the rhythmic clopping of the hooves of cavalry horses on asphalt streets, accompanied by the merry, metallic jingling of harness and accoutrement.

They heard the heavy trundling roll of artillery pieces hauled by half tracks and motor lorries, and later the characteristic clanking rumble and thunder of the tanks. Music never ceased now. Fife and drum calls interspersed with the brass of the military bands, to be replaced by the drone and squeal of the pipers, or the bugles and kettle-drums of Lancer or Hussar.

Sometimes there would be a pause and to the listeners penetrated the *whap-whap-WHAP* of arms being grounded as the parade came to a temporary halt. Then the cries of the officers would come floating across, fading into the distance, each command igniting the one behind it. Again there would be the slap and rattle of rifles being shouldered, another mournful call and the threshing rhythm of trained feet stepping in unison.

In this manner, regiment by regiment, the sounds made by the armed might of Great Britain and the Commonwealth on parade crested the wall, while overhead the bombers and fighters of the Air Force added their blasting, crackling roar of the fly-past to the grand military symphony.

And through it all a small boy, hidden and unnoticed by those packed closely about him, endured torment unspeakable.

For this was what Johnny Clagg had come for, a glimpse of those uniformed and glittering marchers on the other side of the barrier. For this he had willingly surrendered his cherished holiday. Never again during his childhood would all of the soldiers, sailors and airmen of what had once been the greatest empire the world had known be gathered to march together.

They were passing by now, steel-helmeted, pith-helmeted, bearskin-topped, capped or cuirassed, in uniforms of white, blue, green, khaki or scarlet with skins of every shade from northern white to golden tan to tropic black.

Besides the smashing British regiments where Johnny's heart lay, there would be Fiji and Solomon Islanders, brown men from Borneo, Jamaica, Ceylon, Malay and Somaliland, regiments from Sarawak, the Bahamas, Kenya and Pakistan and the West, East and South of Africa. He should be looking upon contingents from Hong-Kong, Papua, New Guinea, Australia, New

Zealand, Canada and Rhodesia. When ever again would a boy be able to gaze upon the famous green-uniformed Gurkhas with their *kukris*, or the red coats and stetsons of the equally famous North-West Mounted Police?

With them would be rolling the mechanical monsters to enchant the heart of a boy, all the enthralling hardware of war: howitzers with black, gaping mouths, anti-aircraft cannon pointing admonishing fingers to the sky, Long Tom rifles capable of hurling an atom charge, machine-gun and mortar batteries, Bren-carriers, half tracks, field and mountain artillery, flame- and rocket-throwers, and the great land battleships, the monster tanks. All these were passing by now while Johnny stood silent and shivering in the cold and rain.

Will Clagg dared not look at his son. Another day, he promised himself, he would take him to the pictures, where he would see in colour, to be sure, what he was missing now. Yet the father knew that it wouldn't be the same, could never be the same for the child as seeing it accompanied by all the noise and thundering of reality.

And if his son was suffering, what must yet be endured by the child who touched his heart the most, for whom he had the softest feeling because she was his daughter? What could he do when the time came for which he knew she waited – the passing of the Queen? What would he say to her? For over a month, ever since the trip had been planned, her whole life and being had been bound up with the excitement of this moment.

Now he felt his own anguish to be almost unbearable.

He was holding his daughter in his arms at this point, her head resting on his shoulders, and he risked a glance at her. Her eyes were open, but her thoughts, he could see, were turned inwards as they so often did when she would retire from the external world. It was as though she knew that none of this crashing and bashing and zinging and tootling had anything immediate to do with her desire. The Queen – *her* Queen – was still far off. She was waiting.

It was shortly before four o'clock in the afternoon when the miserable rain which had been pelting down all the day stopped. Rents appeared in the heretofore solid, gloomy, grey canopy of cloud, and the sun showed itself intermittently. The skies lightened and so did the spirits of all. The momentary appearance of the sun, the instant of pallid warmth upon the cheek, was accepted almost as an omen. Surely this was a harbinger of better things and times to come? Yet the barrier remained firmly closed.

A new sound intruded; made itself felt as well as heard. It began like that distant compact roaring that one hears when one puts one's ear to a sea-shell, but rising in pitch and intensity, swelling in volume and coming ever nearer. The Queen was approaching at last. It was the time her schedule called for her golden carriage to pass Hyde Park Corner. And the greater the crescendo of the nearing torrent of cheers the more quiet fell upon those still remaining behind the wooden barrier, as every ear strained to hear what could not be seen.

The great tidal wave of sound poured up Piccadilly, its crest leaped Wellington Place and echoed from the buildings of Hyde Park Corner and Knightsbridge. And against the background of this awesome flood another sound could now be distinguished, the steel-shod tread of heavy horses and the rumble of a great lumbering spring-less coach.

At that point Gwenny began to scream, 'Daddy, Daddy, she's coming! I can't see! I can't see anything!'

Flesh, blood and a human soul could bear no more. Will Clagg shouldered his way to the foot of the barrier and the young constable standing there. 'God's truth, man, ain't you got no 'eart? This baby's travelled nearly two hundred miles sitting up all night to see the Queen. Stand aside before I knock you there!'

Roaring cataracts of sound overwhelmed the clatter of the approaching golden coach, engulfing them all. Pierced by the anguished crying of the child, confused and worried, the constable braced himself for trouble. Now under duress and threat of violence it was impossible for him to give in and let them through. The wave of cheering that was shaking the earth unnerved and rattled him further; he stood erect, throwing his arms across the door, barring it.

Will Clagg made a fist like a knotted club and drew it back, when he felt his elbow caught and a voice at his ear said, ' 'Ere now, mate, take it easy. Knocking P.C.s about will get you nothing, We'll fix up the kiddy. Give us a leg up on to your shoulder.'

Clagg hardly saw the fellow. He was someone in a fawn mackintosh with a cloth cap pulled down over his face to keep out the rain. There was a pair of eyes and a bit of scrubbly moustache, and then he found that he had cupped his hands and the man had put a foot in and with the ease of a gymnast had swung himself up on to his shoulders, whence he leaned down and called, 'Now then, boost up the girly! Give us your hand there, luv. That's it! Up she goes. Just like a front seat at the Palladium!'

They were three high now, like acrobats in a circus, except that Gwenny was able to steady herself by gripping his head while the stranger held her legs firmly on his shoulders. Gwenny was now two heads higher than the wall and able to look over it at the bewildering kaleidoscope of colour and movement on the other side.

From beneath, applause and a cheer went up with cries of 'Well done! Good work! That's more like it! What about that, constable?'

The policeman merely stood there looking sheepish; he could recall nothing in the regulations about this and, besides, he didn't wish to; he was relieved to be clear of the situation for the moment.

Over the vast sea of heads now frothed with waving handkerchiefs, flags and pennants, Gwenny stared and stared. Her little mouth was open and her pale cheeks flushed. Once she raised her hand tentatively and waved it.

Below, the others, and among them Granny Bonner, were shouting and cheering and waving just as though they were actually seeing the Queen go by and could be seen by her. Violet Clagg was weeping again, both with emotion and disappointment. Somehow even she had not been able to believe that the day could go so utterly and hopelessly wrong.

Clagg had made himself into a foundation of steel supporting the two on his shoulders, but his heart was soft with gratitude. A small piece of prayed-for miracle was happening. He had made a mess of things, he, Will Clagg, who too had dreamed of paying homage to the Queen. He had got himself imprisoned like a huge booby behind a wooden wall. But at least one promise had been kept. His daughter was no longer blind.

From her vantage-point Gwenny turned for a moment and looked down upon her mother, granny and brother. Her eyes were enormous and filled with wonder. The streaks of tears were still on her cheeks, but she no longer wept. Someone called up from below, 'What's she like?'

The child said, 'I saw her.'

Another voice said, 'That's nice. Tell us about it.' And someone else laughed.

'She waved to me,' Gwenny announced. She turned back once more to view the scene and suddenly began to wave her hand wildly, though at what or whom nobody could tell. The cheering was already beginning to spread northwards along the road leading through Hyde Park.

'Hoy!' the same voice which had enquired before shouted up from below. 'What's happening now?'

Gwenny's eyes were now even larger with excitement. She called down, 'There was another one who waved to me, but she was fat and all black like my Topsy.' Somebody murmured the name of Queen Salote and there was more laughter.

In the excitement of the moment everyone had forgotten about Johnny Clagg, a small nondescript boy in a too long navy-blue mackintosh (Granny's idea so that he could grow into it) stained dark with the day's rain, his soggy school cap perched on the back of his head. There he stood, half-pint size, two eyes, two ears, a nose and mouth atop a soaked, coloured scarf, compelled to watch his younger sister favoured, hoisted to a vantage-point from whence she could see the Queen and everything else that was going on.

Yet he had hardly noticed Gwenny being lifted up to the top of the barrier, for with the burst of cheering and the rumbling of the golden coach that heralded the approach of the Queen, Johnny Clagg had departed astrally from his envelope and from the side of Granny and his mother. He had melted through the barrier, changed his costume and now, clad in cuirass and helmet with chin-strap, with shining sword at his shoulder, he rode a coal-black steed as Captain Clagg of Her Majesty's Household Cavalry in

71

command of the troops riding beside and protecting the golden coach.

Keen eyes alert, all of the senses including the sixth keyed up to the occasion and his responsibilities, Captain Clagg was prepared and ready for any eventuality.

Hah! What was that? A sudden stir! A movement in the front rank of the crowd at the kerbside! An arm and a hand pointing something that glittered in the sun that had just broken through the clouds, and above it a face with dishevelled hair, wild rolling eyes and a broken, snaggle-toothed grin!

A maniac! An assassin! The pistol aimed full at the royal pair as they drove by. Faster than lightning was the movement with which brave, vigilant Captain Clagg hurled himself from his horse. A mad howl from the crazed killer, a flash, a report! Slowly Captain Clagg sank to the pavement. The bullet intended for the Queen had lodged in his breast. The maniac was struggling in the hands of the police, but the danger was over. The Queen was saved!

But Captain Clagg knew that his wound was mortal. Already kind hands had raised him to a sitting position and a doctor, kneeling at his side with his little black bag, was shaking his head saying, 'Alas, there is little we can do for him.'

The crowd about him suddenly stirred and broke, and Captain Clagg heard cries of 'Make way! Make way for Her Majesty the Queen!'

And the next moment the Queen herself in her silver gown, the gold- and diamond-studded crown upon her head, and still clutching her golden sceptre, was kneeling at his side and pillowing his head upon her breast, unmindful of his life's blood ebbing away through his wound.

He heard her low, sweet voice throbbing with suppressed emotion, querying, 'What is the name and rank of this brave man who has yielded up his life for mine?'

The next moment there was the Duke of Edinburgh bending over him too, saying, 'Gallant Captain, noble soldier! You have saved my wife; you have saved the Queen; you have saved the nation!'

Captain Clagg gazed upward into the exquisite eyes of his monarch, from whence a tear fell and splashed upon his cheek. A Queen's tear! More priceless than any diamond in her crown. 'I die happy, Your Majesty,' breathed Captain Clagg.

A herald in stiff tabard resplendent with scarlet and gold made his way through the crowd and, drawing himself up, announced, 'Your Majesty! In obedience to your command I have been able to ascertain the following: that brave man who lies dying there is none other than Captain John Clagg, formerly of the Primary School, Little Pudney, Sheffield. His proud parents are William and Violet Clagg. Mr Clagg is connected in an executive capacity with the No. 2 Furnace of the Pudney Steel Works. He also has a grandmother, a Mrs Bonner, who was always predicting that he would come to no good end. How she will rue her words when she hears of his noble sacrifice, for had it not been for his keen eye and quick wit Your Majesty would have been —'

The herald could proceed no further, for he was overcome with emotion at the contemplation of the terrible tragedy that had been averted.

The Queen now arose and from her breast she removed the blue riband and diamond star of the Order of the Garter and laid it on Captain Clagg's form. Then with her golden sceptre she touched his shoulders while she spoke these ringing words, 'No, by my troth! Plain Captain Clagg no longer. Die if you must, then, gallant soldier, for Elizabeth the Second and your country, but die *Captain Lord Clagg, First Baron Pudney*!'

Someone in the crowd now proposed three cheers for His Lordship and they were given with a will. The Queen bent over and tenderly kissed his brow, while her royal consort pressed his hand. Captain Clagg felt his senses swim with joy!

At this point Johnny became aware that his mother was tugging at his hand, breaking into the quandary in which he found himself as to whether he should go on and die decently, as apparently they all expected him to do, and have a tombstone with a fine inscription – 'Saviour of the Queen' – set up over his grave, or whether he should recover miraculously to continue life as Baron Pudney, favourite of the Queen.

74

'Shout, Johnny!' cried his mother. 'The Queen is coming by! God bless and save our gracious Queen!'

The sweetness of the daydream faded. Grown-ups were always breaking into one's reveries. Lord Clagg of Pudney was filed away for future adventures when he should be alone in his bed at night, and Johnny shouted dutifully, 'God save the Queen! Hurrah for the Queen!' He was back behind the barrier again, a wet, hungry, tired, trampled upon, disappointed Johnny Clagg who had come all the way from Sheffield for nothing. He remembered then that there would be no summer holiday either, no shrimping along the sand, no building of beach castles, no exploration of tidal pools in the rocks, no roundabouts, not anything. He turned his face away so that the others would not see and commenced quietly to cry.

The hoof-clatter of the great percherons and the rumble of the royal coach were no longer to be heard. They had given way to the clippety-clop and a dry rolling of lighter carriages. The wave of cheering in the vicinity had likewise receded; it had raced ahead along the tree-lined avenue of East Carriage Drive and could be heard thundering in the distance.

Gwendoline turned around and said, 'I want to get down.' Hands reached up to help. She slid down the frame of the stranger and that of her father until her feet touched the ground. Then she ran to her mother and threw her arms about her and buried her face in her skirt.

The man still perched on Clagg's shoulders didn't yet

himself attempt to descend. Instead he called down to Johnny Clagg, 'Hoy, young feller, what about a look-see for you?'

Johnny shook his head and kept his face turned away from them. It was not dignified to go crawling up a stranger to sit on his shoulders. It was all right for Gwenny, who was a little girl, but not for him, and particularly as he was aware of a small lingering residue of his beautiful day-dream, not the thing for Lord Clagg, First Baron Pudney. And besides, it was too late. All the soldiers would have gone by. Johnny, keeping his face averted, shook his head again. The man placed his hands on Will Clagg's shoulders and leaped lightly to the ground.

'Thanks,' said Will Clagg and stuck out his hand. His legs were weary to the point of exhaustion from the weight, but he was filled with such a turmoil of emotion and gratitude that he could find no more to say. He was aware of an unthinkable impulse to embrace the non-descript-looking stranger with the pulled down cap and scrubbly moustache and call him brother. Instead he could only repeat, 'Thanks,' and then said, 'If you ever find yourself Little Pudney way, outside Sheffield —'

'Oh, that's all right,' the stranger replied. 'I didn't want to see you get into trouble. I could tell you were from the North.' He nodded with his head in the direction of the constable. 'That clot isn't a London copper. Glad to oblige.'

There was an instant's commotion from inside the

barrier, and all those who still remained outside stirred once more as though perhaps there was to be a reprieve in the last moment for them to see at least the tail end of what was going by. From within, a whole section of the barrier gate was swung open, sufficiently to let a horseman through.

He was the most magnificent, awesome and inspiring figure that Johnny Clagg had ever seen. He was dressed in a navy-blue uniform frogged and piped with black, as were the stripes upon his sleeve. Rows of medals and coloured ribbons gleamed upon his breast and on his shoulders were golden epaulets. His face, stern, rugged, aquiline, reminded Johnny of pictures he had seen of the Duke of Wellington at Waterloo. His hair was silver grey and on his head was perched a black cocked hat from which tumbled a cascade of gallant white rooster feathers. He was mounted on an exquisite white mare. She had a pink nose and anxious eyes. The dark skirts of the coat of his uniform fell on either side of her flanks. His black boots were gold-spurred.

Johnny Clagg saw him first as a vision through his tears and then, as he hastily wiped them away, more clearly as a gorgeous apparition in a uniform he didn't recognise, and he prided himself that he could identify on sight every regiment in the United Kingdom. But he was not a Lancer nor a Hussar, not a Dragoon nor a member of the Household Cavalry. Yet in his person and his bearing he embodied all that Johnny had come to see that day. The uniform which Johnny failed to recognise marked him as an Assistant Commissioner of the Metropolitan Police.

Hardly aware of what he was doing, Will Clagg stepped forward and placed his hand upon the horse's bridle and heard himself shouting, 'What's it to be? Are you letting us in or aren't you?' He had been roused beyond control by the age-old antagonism between the man on foot looking up and the man on horseback looking down. If to the son the figure epitomised all the glamour and splendour and power and command, to the father he stood for the arrogance of privilege, the lord against the peasant. The outburst was pure atavism.

Appalled, the constable on guard at the small door leaped for Will with a 'Here, here!' but the Assistant Commissioner held up his hand to stop him from seizing the man at his bridle. From the vantage of his perch on his white horse he could look down into the cluster of anxious, angry, tear-stained human faces, and guess at once that at hand was what might be called a situation.

'What is the trouble here, constable?' he asked. The calm courtesy of his voice brought Clagg to his senses and he let go the bridle and stepped back.

'They've been badgering me all day to let them through, sir,' the constable said. 'Orders were to let no one in without proper credentials. I've only tried to do my duty, sir.'

He was young, he was nervous, he was from the country, he had never in his life seen such a high police official. He visualised himself with his career suddenly broken or ruined. It was incidents like these, if one did the wrong thing, that could finish a man in the Force.

'Badgering he calls it,' protested Will Clagg. 'What about all the others standing here in the rain since morning? What about the kiddies here come to see the Queen and the soldiers? What about your dirty ticket swindles that you coppers don't do anything to stop? Fifty quid of my hard-earned money on a hole in the ground and that young whipper-snapper there talking about his duty!'

The Assistant Commissioner was a perceptive man who had the knack of reconstructing from but a few facts and hints. He knew enough about counterfeit tickets that day to guess that here probably was a victim. And he saw, too, all the dread and terror in the face of the young constable. And to himself the Commissioner made a judgement upon him: *Poor chap, he'll never go far in this business. He has no flexibility.* And looking down upon Clagg and the all too familiar family – the wife with the worried eyes, the inevitable grandmother and the children – he wished that the constable had had the courage, the humanity and the rebelliousness in his nature to be derelict in his duty and to have let them through. However, what he said was, 'You were quite right, constable. Orders were meant to be obeyed.' And then silently and inwardly to himself: *And thick-headed, conscientious young constables must be upheld in the performance of their duty according to the letter, or their world would crash about their ears.* Aloud he said to the stocky man standing close to the pink muzzle of his horse, the man who looked like an iron worker or a steel puddler so nearly made of steel himself, 'I am sorry, the constable had his orders. Had he ignored them he would have risked a reprimand.'

The constable was not so dense that he didn't hear the word 'risk', and he looked up quickly into the face of the Assistant Commissioner to see whether blame or censure was implied, but there was no clue to be found in the grave expression of the dignitary and he comforted himself with the fact that he had been upheld in his actions, and after all done what he had been told to do.

So there, then, was an end to the incident, one minor one of more than a hundred that had occupied the official from early morning that day, and, being at an end, it was already out of his mind when the Assistant Commissioner suddenly was aware of his gaze becoming entangled with that of the small boy who belonged to the family involved. Thus he found himself looking into a young, pale, tear-stained face beneath a sodden school cap, from which were regarding him two dark, luminous, worshipping eyes.

It all happened so quickly that when it was over and he was trotting his horse into the Park, the Assistant Commissioner could no longer remember what it was he had seen in them. He only knew that somewhere he had been deeply touched, and, unable to disengage himself from the child, he had done something he had never meant to do. This was to reach into a pocket deep in the skirts of his uniform coat and take out a shining regimental badge – a crown whereon were intertwined the initials 'RW' with lion and unicorn rampant on either side and the motto of the regiment in Latin, the single word *FIDELIS*.

It must have fallen from the cap of an officer during the procession and the feet of marching men had kicked it to the gutter in Piccadilly. Its momentary glitter in the fitful sun, which had emerged when the downpour ceased, had caught his eyes and he had halted his horse for a moment to peer down at it. An alert constable who had noted this came over at once, picked it up and gave it to him. It was the badge of a famous British regiment, the Royal Wessex. Several of its officers frequented the same club as the Assistant Commissioner. He had slipped it into his pocket with a smile. He saw himself handing it across the bar to one of them between drinks; a silly, innocent enough fantasy which amused him.

But instead of this he had now withdrawn it from his pocket, leaned down from his horse and said to the unknown small boy, 'Here then, lad, have this!' And then had added, 'It is the badge of the Royal Wessex.'

Yet there was one thing he remembered clearly as he rode away, and that was the last expression in the no longer troubled eyes as the boy had held the object in his fingers. It was the look of bottomless gratitude and a kind of shuddering awe of one who has shared in a miracle.

Now why on earth did I do that? The Assistant Commissioner mused to himself, and, not finding any answer, put the matter out of his head.

'What a nice kind gentleman,' Violet Clagg said. 'What is it he gave you, Johnny?'

'Nothing,' said Johnny Clagg, and stuffed it hard down into his trouser-pocket, his hand gripping it so fiercely that the metal cut into his flesh. He had called it nothing because it was everything – a talisman or a symbol of all he ever wanted, or cared about, or wished for, or hoped to be. He was already so passionately jealous of it that he was cold with terror that they would try to take it away from him, that somehow Granny would find some excuse for meddling.

Indeed, she did say, 'More clutter, I'll wager,' but was distracted when the young constable, grateful for his escape, yet still aware that all had not gone off exactly too well, and that for some reason he didn't understand the dignitary had conferred a benefice upon one of the party, announced, 'That was an Assistant Police Commissioner,' and then added, glancing at his watch, 'The procession will be over soon. You'll be able to get through then.'

Still another band went blaring by on the other side. Fiercely clutching his badge, Johnny Clagg no longer cared, for by the thing in his possession he had been made a part of it all.

'Thanks for nothing,' Will Clagg said. 'Fat lot of good that will do us.'

At last they realised that there was no more music, no more tramp of marching feet. A police sergeant stuck his head through the door and said something to the constable which wakened him, got him off the one-way track on which his mind had been set, which was to keep everybody out. Now he had to make an announcement, 'Stand back, please. Everybody stand back, please. The gates are about to be opened. You'll have to make room, please.'

Then there was a groaning and creaking of wood and the whole of the barrier parted in the centre and was swung wide, to loose such a torrent of humanity as threatened to engulf and carry away all those who had remained there. The parade was over, the fun was finished, and now this vast throng which had enjoyed the spectacle developed one powerful mass-will, which was to get away from there to go home, to get warm, to eat, to drink, to spend pennies, and their coming was like a cattle stampede.

The Clagg family formed a small islet against this tide with Will opposing his sturdy bulky form to the onrush, around which it broke and swirled. Several other parties who had stood there too were trying to move in the opposite way and for the same reason. They had been there all day, straining to go in a certain direction, frustrated by a wooden wall, forbidden by fear of the law, and now that both of these barriers were removed they were determined to continue in that desired direction. Some hoped to reach the Palace, only to encounter a solid wall of humanity several yards deep blocking them. So they simply kept pushing against those trying to leave.

The shoulders that banged into his, and the angry faces of those he thumped with his increasingly truculent opposition, provided Will Clagg with the first satisfaction he had experienced that day. It had been impossible to crash and demolish the barrier and not too clever to think of bashing a constable or two, but he could oppose himself to these unthinking, unseeing people who, having had their fun, were now trying to run over him. He could thump them and bump them and make them feel the presence of Will Clagg of Little Pudney. He was without knowing it undergoing the very necessary process of regaining some of the manhood he had lost.

Soon Clagg found that there was no longer anyone to bump or bash or shoulder out of the way. The approach to the Palace was hopeless with the tide of humanity flooding the drive, backwashing almost to the entrance of the Park. They were walking along where the procession had passed, and approaching Piccadilly.

From the direction of Constitution Hill came a mighty roar and Clagg guessed that the Queen must be coming up the Mall. From off in the distance snatches of military music still came to them, wind-wafted. Somewhere the spectacle was continuing; flags and pennants waved; marching men were passing by; wine was being drunk. But where the Clagg family now found themselves amidst the rapidly dispersing remainder of the crowd were only lees and dregs of the glory that had been.

Underfoot were horse-droppings flattened out and all the debris that massed humans leave behind them: paper in which sandwiches had been wrapped, discarded souvenirs, rosettes, squashed celluloid dolls, broken sticks of flags too lustily waved, handkerchiefs, cigarette-butts and cigar-stubs. For Johnny there was a momentary interest in the tank-tracks imprinted into the road like spoors of some gigantic prehistoric monsters. Here they had passed by.

The wet bunting hung plastered to the wooden stands. The windows on the north side of the street, which had been filled with partying spectators, were now emptied so that the bare planks on which they had sat showed like bones. No one had yet bothered to begin to clean up the litter they had left behind them. What a view those who had sat there must have had! Motor traffic and the first buses allowed through came roaring down Piccadilly, bulging with people. The city was beginning to pick up its normal routine of life externally, but within doors and throughout the country the celebrations would continue far on into the night and the following morning.

And there in the middle of the street Clagg's offensive ground to a halt. The fire went out of him and he was once more without purpose. 'Ought we go look at some of the decorations?' he asked.

'I've seen all the decorations I want to see for the rest of my life,' Granny snapped.

'I'm hungry,' said Johnny.

'I'm thirsty,' said Gwendoline.

'I'm tired,' said Violet. 'Oughtn't we try to get some-thing to eat for the children?'

'Come along then,' Clagg said, rather satisfied to have

matters taken out of his hands again. 'We'll find a pub or a Lyons somewhere and all have something hot.' He picked Gwenny up in his arms again and moved off down Piccadilly, for he knew enough about London to know that beyond Piccadilly Circus was the area of cafés and snack bars.

They had, of course, not reckoned upon the fact that a million or so starved and dehydrated citizens would have the same idea. Every restaurant, Corner House and bar was jammed to the doors, with long queues waiting outside. Eventually, after a long wait and standing up at a counter, they managed to connect with a cup of lukewarm tea and a bun, which did little either for their stomachs or their morale. In the café someone was talking about the fireworks display there would be on the river that night opposite the Embankment; others discussed a celebration to be held at Wapping Town Hall; somewhere in the East End a huge street party had been arranged; north, east, south and west, high and low, London was preparing for a night of celebration.

Will Clagg looked at his tired family and knew that he must get them home and himself as well. Beaten and dispirited, there was nothing left in him but the desire to retire as quickly as possible to the security of the four walls of his house, where he could close the door upon this outside world which had so let him down; home, whose sheltering familiarity could be pulled about one's bruised shoulders. The necessity to set his foot once more upon his own threshold became compelling, overwhelming.

A policeman put them right as to the proper bus for St Pancras. Four went by before the queue in which they had to stand melted sufficiently to permit them to embark. They were too tired even so much as to glance at the decorations or shop windows or the teeming London streets during the ride.

St Pancras was a damp, pulsating, squalid turmoil, a compendium of the smell of soggy clothing, coal smoke, sausages, beer, wet boots and tea. Always there was the sound of panting locomotives, one of which emitted an occasional agonised shriek of terror at the thought of its impending task of drawing its heavy load of humans.

One heard the clanking of couplings, the ring of bells, the piping of the guards' whistles, the rumble of the porters' barrows and, as always on that day, the endless shuffling of thousands upon thousands of now weary feet. The babble of human voices arose against the hot hissing of discharged steam. In the dark, glass-covered, iron-ribbed cavern of the station all the sounds multiplied and echoed hollowly.

Throngs pushed and struggled, whirligigged and gravitated towards the gates leading to the long sooty trains which would carry them northwards to their distant homes. Like colonies of ants of different species the streams collided, formed knots and clustered and sorted themselves out again as their members found their way into their proper channels. There was much crowding and shoving, but these were people of high spirits. In one way or another each of them had had some contact with the miracle of continuity which had been enacted in the Abbey that day. England again had a young queen. Her being and her crowning likewise pointed up and set the seal upon this same continuity of themselves. They too had come down with her in that long unbroken line from the dark and buried past into the brilliant and thrilling present.

Later on that night the assault of the home-going mobs upon transportation was to become more desperate, less good-tempered, wilder and out of all proportion in numbers to the available space on trains or station platforms. But at that hour of half-past six there were not yet so many, only the early birds with a long way to go, or the sensible ones who were passing up the fireworks and a tour of the illuminated decorations in favour of a more comfortable passage homeward. Still, the station was jammed, but cheerfully so and passable. And through the ruck Will Clagg steered his family in the direction of the 6.58 Midland Express.

Like the others, they fought and thrust and pushed their way against counter-thrusts and counter-pushes, propelling, whirling and batting them from all sides until at last they fell or were sucked into the colony of their brother and sister ants all bound in the same direction, and thereafter progress was automatic. Through the gates, down the platform, into the empty and waiting compartments, and there, by virtue of their decision to be early, all five found seats, Johnny and Gwendoline by the window, Will and Elsie and Violet by their sides. With a great sigh of relief, they sagged or moulded themselves into the stiff bristles of the grimy carriage seats and backs. They had not realised how tired they were.

Young Johnny's place was on the platform side of the carriage, and, as he looked out of the window at the seemingly endless streams of people pouring into the trains, a gleam of excitement replaced the fatigue in his young eyes at the sight of the occasional uniform of a soldier, red or green or blue in the drab of the crowd. His right hand was pressed deep into his trouser-pocket, clutching his talisman, and his index finger wandered about the contours of the wonderful metal badge, now hot from contact with his flesh. He felt the initials, the crest, the lion and the unicorn rampant. He would have liked to have drawn it forth to inspect it, to have added the testimony of his eyes to the fact that it was really there and his very own to keep for ever. But he felt that if he did so now one of his family would be sure to ask to see it. They might even take it from him. It would have to wait until he was alone.

Gwendoline was dreaming with her hands in her lap. Whatever the dream was, it curled the corners of her mouth with mystery. Her eyes were sleepy, but there was a hint of wonder in them.

Grandma Bonner had quietly come apart with old age and fatigue approaching exhaustion. She was collapsed in her seat, unmindful of the three strangers who had piled in to conclude the eight of the compartment. Untidy wisps of her hair were straggled over her eyes; her spectacles had slipped down; the colour of her face was grey and ashen; she looked ten years older than she was.

Violet Clagg's countenance was a mirror of the bitterness and apathy that had overwhelmed her in the warmth of the compartment. She had taken off her shoes and sat listening to the ache of her feet as well as to those voices of despondency and surrender that were whispering that it was always like this; it had always been, it always would be. Things never turned out as promised or advertised. Yet one never ceased to be taken in by the promises or broken by the disillusionments.

It was nothing new for Will Clagg to have been on the go from early morn till dusk; there was no complaint from his iron muscles, though the soft of the seat felt good under his hams, but the canker of the fiasco continued to gnaw him. Try as he would, there was no escape from the abysmal failure of the day, the loss of his money, his prestige as head of the family, and, above all, the pain caused by the disappointment of his children.

His mind searched for and brought up the small ameliorating incidents that had happened. There was that badge so strangely handed to Johnny by the high official on the white horse and which in some way had appeared to compensate the boy for the loss of the sight of the procession. And Gwenny seemingly had seen something that had satisfied her – perhaps indeed the Queen. But for himself there was only remembering that he had been a trusting fool, and as husband, father and son-in-law had let all of them down. He felt himself weakened as a man, and worried whether it would show on the broad earth floor of the rolling mill when the furnace gates were opened and the glowing metal was poured. He wondered whether the men under his command would notice it.

On the way from the street to the train Clagg had managed to pick up the evening papers, and now, in an attempt to escape from these self-recriminations which filled him, he leafed through to see in black and white all that they had missed that day in life and colour.

He turned page upon page of pictures: Grenadiers, Life Guards, Horse Guards, Dragoons, Scots, Irish and Welsh. There were Indian troops in turbans, Africans in fezzes, officers on chargers, potentates in carriages, the young Queen crowned in the Abbey, peers paying homage. The colour of the newsprint was the colour of ashes, like the taste of the day left in his mouth.

Clagg turned to the text to try to drive other thoughts from his head and read the account of the morning's happenings, or rather only half read them. The gnawing of the worm, it seemed, could not be ignored.

Yet in the next moment he did find his attention caught as, his eyes passing over the surface of a column headed 'Coronation Miscellany', he came upon the following item:

'Petty thievery, pilfering, and the minor rackets of spivdom were held to a minimum by alert flying squads, according to Detective-Inspector Magillevray of the Metropolitan Police. Nevertheless, pickpockets flourished in certain areas where crowds were the thickest. Several stores were looted and counterfeit tickets to the Abbey, as well as to certain well placed positions on the route of procession, were much in evidence.

'One of the nastiest of such swindles to come to the attention of the police were tickets sold at twenty-five guineas for a window-seat with breakfast, lunch and champagne at an address in Wellington Crescent, which turned out to be nothing but a bombed-out site. Among those who had bought tickets to this non-existent house were Sir Nigel and Lady Alladryn of Perth, Australia – Sir Nigel, who is Chairman of the West Australia Linseed Oil Company, arrived in London late and secured the fake tickets at the last minute from a stranger in the lobby of his hotel – Mr and Mrs Marshall Fess, American millionaires of Sioux Falls, Idaho, and William Clagg, Executive Foreman of the Pudney Steel Mills, Great Pudney, Sheffield, and his family.

'Police working on the case have seized upon the superior engraving and printing of the fake tickets as a clue in their search for those responsible for them. "They would have fooled anyone," said Detective-Sergeant Hayes in charge of the enquiry, "but we hope to be able to report progress before very long." '

'Violet! Granny!' Will Clagg's voice was hoarse with excitement. 'I've got my name in the paper. Look here! Here it is! We weren't the only ones who got stung. Sir Somebody or Other got it too. The Inspector said anybody could have been fooled.'

That wakened them out of their lethargies and self-pities and disappointments, and the two women leaned across the compartment to look where Clagg had his finger and, marvelling, read his name there, 'William Clagg' – the reporter had seen fit to promote him to keep company with the nobleman and the millionaire – '*Executive* Foreman of the Pudney Steel Mills.'

The children, too, pushed close to see, and then the other three passengers in the compartment, a husband and wife and a travelling salesman.

Will Clagg suddenly found himself suffused with a strange and wild exultation, and in his breast a curious sensation of sweetness. He had been touched unexpectedly by the divine lightning of publicity; fifty-three years of anonymity had been dispelled. William Clagg, Executive Foreman of the Pudney Steel Mills – there he was in black print on white paper in the *Evening Standard*. There were similar *Evening Standards* throughout the train no doubt, hundreds of them, and double hundreds of eyes at that moment would be looking upon the account and learning that he was an executive foreman in one of the greatest steel combines in Britain.

And, moreover, he suddenly discovered that he was a

hero. His name was not only linked in a twenty-five-guinea swindle with an Australian knight and an American millionaire, but the fact that he had been a mark and a poor fool was now utterly denied and for ever demolished on the word of no less than Detective-Sergeant Hayes in charge of the case, who had uttered a dictum that the fake tickets would have deceived anyone.

Clagg sat back in the compartment amidst the murmurs of marvel from his family and fellow passengers, and gave himself up to the warm and wonderful feeling that had stolen over him. Now the story of their adventures had to be retold, but somehow it was no longer a tale of disaster and catastrophe, but one of drama which had reached the end it deserved: his name in the papers.

In his mind's eye he already saw himself passing the news item around at the George and Dragon back home, not once but many times. The story would be retold whenever a stranger appeared in the bar or an old friend turned up. The cutting would grow creased and yellow with handling. And perhaps the police *would* return him the counterfeit tickets as they had promised and he would exhibit those along with the bit from the paper. Then visitors would pass their fingers over the gold embossing and agree with Detective-Sergeant Hayes that they might have fooled anyone, as indeed they had, the toffs as well as himself, and goodness knows how many others who had not been so fortunate as to be identified in newsprint.

The grandeur of the revelation lay like a spell upon the

adults in the compartment. Thus it caused them all to jump when the sliding door was ripped open and the uniformed restaurant car attendant thrust his head inside shouting, 'Tickets for dinner, anyone? Only second sitting left —'

The no longer anonymous Executive Foreman of the Pudney Steel Mills raised his square head from the delectable page where his identity stood revealed for all who cared to read, and the sound and import of his own voice astonished him as he said, 'We'll have five, please.'

This brought Granny out of her state of fatigue and shock. 'Will!' she cried. 'Have you lost your senses? Haven't you thrown out enough money as it is? We can have a cup of tea and some biscuits when we get home.'

Violet Clagg said, 'Oh, Will, do you think we ought?' And then sighed, 'I could do with a bite to eat.'

'And a bite of something you shall have, old girl,' said Will Clagg. The urge to celebrate was irrepressible. 'Yes, five for the second sitting,' he repeated. The attendant handed over the tickets.

*

It was perhaps more instinct than intent that had led Clagg to decree that Johnny should occupy a seat at one of the tables for two across the aisle from them in the restaurant car. The father was not entirely unaware of the look of pure, unbelieving bliss that his son bestowed upon him, or the fact that with this gesture he had for ever annulled whatever lingering disappointment might have remained in the boy at the way things had turned out that day. To have a real and proper meal aboard a train roaring at more than a mile a minute through the countryside while there was still light to see out was a treat enough; but to be able to enjoy this by himself at another table, unsupervised, unobserved, unrestricted, so that no limits could be placed upon the soaring of his imagination – this was too good to be true.

The restaurant car consisted of tables for four on one side and smaller ones for two opposite on the other side of the narrow passage through which waiters threaded their way, performing the most incredible balancing acts with trays of food and drink.

Bliss indeed! The table for two opposite where the Claggs – Mum and Dad, Gwenny and Gran – had established themselves was occupied, but there was another two-placer one down from them still empty, and here Johnny seated himself facing the engine, his back to his family and most fortuitously out of their direct line of observation and contact.

Yet this wonderful moment, this unexpected, totally miraculous situation came so close to being blasted. Busybody, fusspot Granny, of course! Johnny had hardly seated himself and taken the menu in his hands when he heard over the rackety-rack and clickety-click of the wheels her querulous voice, 'Ought the boy be there by himself, Will?' He heard his mother say, 'I don't know, Granny,' and then didn't hear his father's reply, only Granny's continued plaintive note.

The iridescent bubble of the wonderful projected dreams he meant to enjoy during the course of the meal he was about to consume now as Major John Clagg, M.C., D.S.O. of the Royal Wessex, threatened to burst. Clickety-clack went the wheels. The brown-clad hips of a waiter whizzed past his head at a speed almost faster than that of the train. 'Oughtn't I go and sit with him?' came the insistent voice of Granny.

Young Johnny screwed his eyes closed and took his lip between his teeth. He made hot, sweaty fists with nails digging into his palms, and with all the force of his being he tried to will it not to happen. Oh, please not to let Granny sit opposite him. Her mouth formed into that small, ever disapproving 'o', destroying Major Clagg for ever, making him into only Johnny Clagg, too young to be allowed to sit by himself.

Then there was a darkening shadow and the button of a pepper-and-salt tweed jacket before his eyes and a deep voice rumbled, 'Is this seat occupied, young man?'

'Oh no, please, sir, do have it,' replied Johnny with such entreating earnestness and invitation in his voice that the man looked down upon him in surprise.

The owner of the voice was extraordinarily tall with an absolutely bald skull, the most astonishing shade of pink.

His face seemed to have both the colour and texture of old, weathered parchment but containing most young-looking and piercingly light-coloured blue eyes surrounded by hundreds of fine, tiny wrinkles. His eyebrows were tufted snow-white and aggressive, and he had a moustache still faintly yellow.

'Well now,' said the gentleman, 'that's most kind and polite of you, my boy. Thank you.' And thereupon, with an athletic ease and grace he took the chair opposite.

Johnny for the moment experienced such a giddiness of relief that he thought almost that he was fainting. Although he didn't have eyes in the back of his head, he knew, he just *knew* that behind him and across the aisle Granny had half risen from her seat to come over and carry out her threat. Now it was too late. Major Clagg was safe.

That was a meal that was never to be forgotten. The menu itself was an introduction to a whole new world, a world in which one had a choice. Potage (whatever that was), grapefruit or tomato juice, announced the soup-flecked, gravy-spotted menu card. Fried fillet of plaice, sauce something-or-other, a real foreign word. And then once again one could linger and dally and debate and make up one's mind between steak and kidney pie or roast pork with apple sauce. However was one to decide upon one or the other of these? Cheese and biscuits or a sweet! Ice-cream or apple tart!

And every time the used plate was whisked away and a clean plate set before. Clean knives and forks. Waiters who regarded and addressed him not as a child but as a man. What an adventure!

Even though he could see the trays approaching from afar as the attendants worked their way down the tables, the moment of decision for the main course still caught him undecided and unprepared. And when the server with the steak and kidney pie with the dark, flaky crust came to the table Johnny craved it, and yet across the aisle slices of white pork with brown, crispy crackling were being served. The waiter stood there with his spoon and fork poised and Johnny found himself speechless and looking up helplessly into his face.

The man had children of his own; he understood the problem. 'Can't make up your mind, eh?' he said. Johnny could only nod. 'Have a bit of both, then.' Before Johnny could reply he spooned out a generous portion of steak, crust and kidney, straightened up to murmur something to his colleague, and in the next instant there was a slice of crackling pork and apple sauce on the plate.

Behind the backs of the waiters the family was out of sight and out of range of this marvel. No Granny to veto, no mother to fuss, no sister to be kept quiet. And then to cap the rightness of it all, the old gent opposite said to the attendant, 'Hm, that looks good. I wonder if I might do the same?'

After the main course there came a pause which permitted the meal to settle into place, shaken down nicely from side to side by the swaying of the train. Outside the windows, grimed with coal dust and rain, the twilight was at hand and lights were coming on in the houses, neons blinked in the towns through which they roared, and the headlamps of cars on the roads that sometimes paralleled the track were like the shafts of searchlights.

Yet, oddly, with his new-found freedom which would so soon end Johnny had not yet lost himself in those dreams of grandeur which the adventure had promised. For one thing there had not been time. So much had been happening too quickly. Like many of the diners, he had been caught up by the rhythm of the ballet of the waiters, the sinuosity with which they avoided contact with one another as they glided to and fro, their narrow escapes from collision, clash and disaster, one tray high, one tray low, as they passed each other, accompanied by the music of the wheels over the rails and the shrieks and wails of the locomotive.

And, truth to tell too, there had been something else occupying Johnny's mind. It was the precious badge in his pocket which he could feel firm against his leg. He was experiencing an overwhelming desire to look upon it again and here was his chance, away from his family. Also he found himself entertaining half a wish to show it off before the old gentleman with the tufted eyebrows.

Therefore, he slowly withdrew it from his pocket, holding it in his lap for a moment. Warmth and perspiration had dulled it somewhat and he took his napkin and polished it furiously until it shone again in the lamplight of the restaurant car. Then he put it on the table-cloth beside his plate and looked down, entranced by the beauty and content of it. The regimental badge, insignia of rank, courage and gallantry, lost from the cap of a proud officer, presented to him by a demigod on a white horse because for one moment their eyes had met in a thrall and there had been an understanding, was his.

Old Tufted Eyebrows, too, was staring down at the shining metal and beneath the bald, pink skull there raced a thousand memories. 'Where did you get that, boy?' he rumbled.

Johnny took his gaze from the glittering talisman and looked into the piercing, bright blue eyes of the old gentleman.

'A gentleman – an officer gave it to me, sir.'

'Hm,' said the old gentleman, 'that's very strange. I can't think of an officer who would part with a thing like that. Are you sure? Do you know what that is?'

Johnny replied, 'Yes, sir. It's the badge of the Royal Wessex. I know them all.' And then as understanding of what the old gentleman was driving at dawned on him, 'Oh, it wasn't one of *them* that gave it to me. It was another, but I don't know what *he* was. He was on a white horse and wore a black uniform and there was a white feather in his cocked hat.'

And when he saw how interested the old gentleman was, and the light in his young blue eyes, the story fairly tumbled out of Johnny: the expedition to the Coronation, the false tickets, their attempts to see at least something, his own love for soldiers and his wish to become one, the affair at the barricade, and the plumed, mounted officer who had upheld the policeman in his duty and then so strangely reached into his pocket and presented him with the badge.

His companion listened to the narrative and seemed not at all surprised at it, merely nodding in agreement and saying, 'That might be Archie.' For he was a man of imagination who always saw things in pictures when stories were told to him, and in his mind he was seeing his friend, one of the Assistant Commissioners, as he noticed the glittering object lying in the street after the legions had passed and pocketed it in order to restore it to its regiment.

He saw the eyes of the child wide upon him and corrected, or rather explained himself better. 'I mean Sir Archibald Green, an Assistant Police Commissioner. Did you notice the number of stripes on his sleeve?'

'Four,' replied Johnny.

The old gentleman nodded. 'Well observed. He always rides about on occasions like this getting his nose into everything. That's why things run as smoothly as they do, I imagine.' He picked up the badge and held it in his palm for a moment. Colour came into his face and a certain odd mistiness to his eyes as though he were undergoing some strong emotional turmoil within himself; which indeed he was, namely that of unexpectedly encountering an old and cherished friend under extraordinary circumstances.

'I was with them when I was a young man,' he said. He sighed. 'I miss them.'

Johnny Clagg looked from the insignia reposing in the brown, veined hand to the blue eyes of the tall man. He understood that he and the 'they' represented by the badge had at one time meant a great deal to one another.

'Was there a lot of fighting?' Johnny asked. 'I want to be an officer when I grow up.'

Then came an interruption in the shape of the nagging voice of Granny Bonner, 'Johnny, is that you doing all that talking? Be quiet, you're disturbing the gentleman at his dinner.'

Johnny flushed and turned around to endure the steel-rimmed, spectacled look. Tufted Eyebrows, too, looked across to the table from whence the admonition had come.

Will Clagg, leaning backwards and turning around, took up the refrain. 'I hope he's not bothering you,' he said. 'He's a bit of a talker, that one, when he gets going.'

'No, no, no,' replied the gentleman, 'not at all. We have something in common and are having a most delightful chat.'

For the second time that day Johnny Clagg felt his heart filled to overflowing. He seemed to have entered into a new world, one in which important grown-ups bothered with small boys and their needs.

Satisfied, Clagg returned his attention to his own table; communications were cut; Johnny was once more safe and secure with his new friend. 'Will I be able to be an officer one day?' he asked again of the tall man opposite who still held his badge in the hollow of his hand.

The gentleman looked across at the boy separated from him by no more than a foot or so, and at the same time by a gulf so wide that at one time he would have said it never could be bridged.

In the moment of the small exchange with the group at the other table, the boy had become identified, labelled, classified. There was Mum and Dad, Granny and little sister, and the boy himself, stout oak for the ribs of the gallant ship that was England, but never before material for the quarter-deck.

In his own time, the gentleman remembered, chances for the son of such a family becoming an officer were one in ten million, or perhaps even no chance at all. Yet equally the chances were that in his day he never would have found himself sitting in a railway restaurant car opposite a dirty but endearing small boy who had produced from a grimy pocket the badge of the regiment that had once been his own, and with all the fervour and ambition of youth had demanded to know whether one day he might become an officer of this famous fighting unit.

Yet he knew that his times were no more. Often he had regretted it; now he was pleased. A half a century had elapsed since he, a gentleman, had been made an officer as well. How old could this boy be? Eleven? Twelve? A decade might see him turned into an officer and a gentleman.

That impassable gulf now seemed no wider than the eighteen inches or so of table that separated him from the boy, and the old man's heart was gladdened that this was so. Along with so many millions of others that day, his spirit had been uplifted by the surge of feeling that had swept the country for the Queen who had been crowned. And it was now almost in the name of this young person that he replied to Johnny Clagg, 'Yes, indeed. I believe that you will be, if you wish it strongly enough.'

'Oh, but I do,' said Johnny.

'Then you must never relent,' said the gentleman, and then repeated four times solemnly, 'Never, never, never, never. The wish must always be with you battering at the gates like an army that doesn't know the meaning of defeat. Against such an attack every defence must fail. Do you not agree?'

The glory of being talked to like a man! 'Yes, sir,' said Johnny.

The gentleman nodded his head reflectively. 'Yes, your ambition must always be kept alive within you; the last thing you think about at night before going to sleep, the first thing when you awaken in the morning. Then you will succeed. Luck plays a part, of course, but then you have already been touched by luck.' He sighed, replaced the regimental badge on the table and with the point of one finger edged it towards the boy, but his gaze still rested upon it.

For all of his happiness at what seemed like a prophecy, a

forecast already almost fulfilled, once more something of the emotions experienced by the gentleman communicated itself to the boy.

The waiter came scribbling bills. The gentleman reached into his wallet, paid, and the waiter passed on. Johnny Clagg edged the badge back across the median line of the table into the gentleman's territory. He could not for the life of him understand why he was doing it, or why he was saying, 'Would you like to have it, sir?' He only knew that he must.

The gentleman stiffened and looked at the boy with what might have been taken as an expression of horrified severity, but only because he was so shaken by the gesture. What had led that child to something so generous, loving and touching? He picked up the regimental badge, weighed it in his palm for a moment, and the mistiness was in his eyes again. 'Thank you, no,' he said. 'Yet I think that this is perhaps the finest gift ever offered to me. No, no, keep it, and some day wear it.' And then he arose from the table to his full and grandiose height, and yet not quite as tall; it was as if he had aged just a little. His last words were, 'Keep it polished, lad,' and he turned and walked away.

Granny Bonner called over from the other table, 'Have you wiped your mouth, Johnny?'

*

None of them had ever dined in a restaurant car before and

they were all on edge not to show it and to orient themselves as to how this might differ from tea at the café to which they sometimes treated themselves on a Sunday afternoon. Violet and Gwendoline had the window-seats, Will Clagg sat opposite Granny on the aisle, his back to the engine. As father of the family and organiser of the treat he had gathered to himself all of the literature on the table, the menu and the folder, which was a combination wine-list and prose paean describing the virtues of British Railways.

Granny's small eyes were darting hither and thither, taking in the table set-up, the fish forks and knives by the side of the plate, the paper napkins which grew out of the glasses, and she remained unsubdued. 'Waste, that's what I call it,' she muttered, 'after all the money we've squandered.'

'Now, now, Granny,' Will Clagg soothed, 'what's a few shillings more or less? It's been a hard day. What'll it be, roast pork or steak and kidney pie?'

Violet said, 'Sit up, Gwenny,' for fatigue had set in and the child had begun one of those descents into her chair which threatened to wind up under the table. 'Do you mean they have both?' she asked of her husband.

'It's a proper feed,' said Will. 'Listen to this —' and he read off the menu, item by item.

Gwenny sat up and said, 'Can I have ice cream?'

'I suppose so,' acquiesced her father, which brought a prompt two pennies' worth from Granny.

'Ice cream before going to bed! When I was a girl we

weren't allowed any foolishness like that.' She turned upon Will. 'And what's all this going to cost us, I'd like to know? A fortune, I'll wager.'

Clagg consulted the menu again. 'Seven and six each,' he replied. 'Not too bad. Thirty-seven and six for the five of us.'

'Well, I only hope you've got it,' Granny snapped, 'and what we're going to do until you're paid again goodness knows.'

Will's hand stole quietly to an inside pocket, there to separate and feel the crackle of three one-pound notes, a fund they didn't know about, saved up and held out by him for emergencies. Every penny of the expedition had been weighed and calculated, but Will was a careful man and no fool. The reason he was foreman of the No. 2 furnace was because he did think ahead to possible difficulties and took his precautions in advance so that they should not occur, or if they did he was ready for them. For this reason Clagg had amassed his secret fund and here it was coming in handy.

'What's grapefruit?' asked Gwendoline. 'Can I have grapefruit, Mummy?'

'I should think not,' vetoed Granny. 'Makes the stummick sour. Hot soup is what she needs.'

To Gwendoline the thing called grapefruit, whatever it was, suddenly became highly desirable. 'Mummy,' she wailed, 'I want grapefruit.'

Violet would have liked the child to have had her wish

but didn't have the energy or the gumption to fight against Granny's dictum. 'No, luvvy,' she said weakly, 'don't fuss. Hot soup's better for you.'

Will Clagg looked aside for an instant in irritation at her submission. Must she always be giving in to her mother? Would she never show any stand-up spine? It had always been like that ever since Granny had come to live with them. Why shouldn't the child have what she wanted, just once? It was a party and a treat, wasn't it? Why did they have to go about spoiling it, then, and nagging and disciplining the way they did at home? He was on the point of reversing the hot soup and then decided against it. It just wasn't worth the fuss and the natter, and besides Granny was annoyingly right. After the chill of the rain, hot soup was more like it. But to hide his exasperation he turned his attention once more to the folder in his hand, and saw something which surprised him greatly.

It was the wine-list, where he read: Champagne, Mumm's, – half bottle 15/-, quarter bottle 8/-.

Eight shillings for a drink of champagne! Who would have thought it! Champagne, the best of which one knew cost you two quid a bottle, suddenly was within reach!

Will Clagg stole another sidelong glance at his wife, but this time there was no longer irritation, but instead sympathy and understanding. The name of the champagne on the menu had brought home to him again the personal disappointment she had suffered at the collapse of their day.

For all of the fact that Will was a heavy, thick-set,

powerful brute of a man who had fought his way up from the ranks of men to command them, he had learned something of the little things that tickled women, an extra ribbon on a dress, or some chintz at a kitchen window. They were not like men; they were more like children. And from the very beginning he had understood that the item which had sold Violet on the whole Coronation scheme and had overcome whatever scruples she might have had, or dissents she could have cooked up, was the champagne, the drink of bubbly advertised with the lunch. He had not, of course, been able to get wholly into her mind and visualise how she saw herself holding the special glass in her hand, the little finger cocked most elegantly, while she contemplated the bubbles rising in the yellow fluid before knocking it back, but he did appreciate that somehow this was to be the focus of the day for her, just that little extra something which sells or captivates a woman.

As he looked now at her features, lined and again pathetically slack after another surrender to her mother, he found his heart touched and filled with a further understanding. In one sense life was an endless string of defeats, frustrations and disappointments. She had never tasted champagne. Her heart had been set upon it and he remembered the wail of anguish that had been torn from her lips as they had faced the empty hole of No. 4 and the grim facts confirmed by the police, 'Then there won't be any bubbly!'

And now beyond the expectation of himself or of them it suddenly lay within his power to remedy this, to rescue something of the shattered day for her with this small delight. Laboriously and yet with commendable speed Will Clagg performed some mental arithmetic within his broad head, based on the prices in the wine-list and a half-a-crown tip at the end, and the answer, double checked, came out right.

The decision coincided with the sudden appearance of the waiter at their table. 'Will there be anything to drink, sir?'

'A quarter bottle of Mumm's champagne.'

The lineaments of the waiter's countenance rearranged themselves to acknowledge the nobility of this order. 'You'll want it iced for a moment, sir, of course.'

'Will Clagg!' Granny almost shouted, completely aghast. 'Have you gone out of your mind?'

He looked at his mother-in-law almost sheepishly as he said, 'What's wrong with a bit of the bubbly for Violet? She's had her mind set on it.'

'Oh, no, Will, I couldn't,' said Violet, almost in terror, for it did seem as though her husband had been robbed of his senses.

'Shut up, luv,' he said, not unkindly, and then, turning to Granny, fired an armour-piercing shot at her, 'What about a drop of gin for yourself, Gran?'

This was her weakness. She loved her nip of gin. The sudden offer threw her completely out of her stride. It was one thing to protest a useless extravagance proposed for her daughter, it was another to argue against a drop of something which she knew would do her the world of good at the moment. Yet she could not accept it without acquiescing in this champagne folly.

Clagg watched the struggle taking place within her with unconcealed delight, and to increase her dilemma added, 'Double, if you like.'

Granny succumbed, for a moment looking just as weak and foolish as her daughter. 'If you've got the stuff to pay for it, Will, I could do with a bit of warming.'

'A double pink gin,' ordered Clagg. 'I'll have a Bass, and bring the kiddy a ginger-beer and same for the boy over there.'

The waiter wrote it all down carefully, his lips silently forming the words of the order, 'One quart. bott. Mumm's One doub. pink gin. One Bass. Two ginger-beer,' and sailed off, leaving behind him a table in the throes of a sensation.

The dining-car filled up, the train rattled, roared, swayed and bounded, the sounds occasionally augmented from far ahead by the shrill shriek of the engine. In what seemed like even less than a trice, the wine waiter, performing a most graceful and exquisite *pas seul* down the aisle, was back at their table with the tray of bottles. On it was a proper thin-stemmed, wide-mouthed champagne glass and a miniature silver-coloured ice-bucket filled with water, in which floated two discouraged lumps of ice knocking gently against the quarter bottle of Mumm's. Everything was dwarf size, yet a hundred per cent. The cork of the bottle was foil-wrapped and wire-bound; the label was gay and French.

The waiter looked a question at Clagg, who waved a stubby-fingered hand in the direction of his wife. Glass and bucket were set on the table by her. A healthy-looking dollop of angostura-coloured gin was put before Granny and diluted to her taste with water, and then, with a motion like a magician pulling rabbits out of a hat and the blinding speed of the prestidigitator, the waiter decapped the bottle of Bass and the bottles of ginger-beer, poured them half full to allow for the sloshing about they would get from the movement of the express train, and served them. 'Shall I open the champagne now, madam? It was iced before.'

'Yes, please,' replied Violet. Her eyes were like saucers, her lips parted with excitement. She was sitting bolt upright now. Fatigue had departed from her, as it had too from Gwendoline, who, likewise ramrod stiff, had buried her nose in the ginger-beer.

The waiter was a wise, wry, trained man. He had catalogued the group at the table in an instant, twigged the festive champagne, and meant to stint nothing of proper ceremony.

He had a napkin over his arm. Plucking the tiny bottle from the bucket, he swadled it like a child in the cloth, then his nimble fingers twisted the wire until it was loose enough to remove and laid it carefully on the table next to the bucket. He knew it would vanish from thence as a souvenir. He tested the cork once secretly with strong fingers, and hoped for their sake that it would pop. So often these little splits were flat and the cork came out as from a medicine bottle. No, there was some tension there. He screwed twice and then pulled, and even above the noise of the train there was an adequately gratifying explosion, and several heads were turned satisfyingly in their direction, as happens irresistibly anywhere champagne is opened.

A bubble of froth at once appeared at the mouth of the green glass bottle, but the experienced and knowing waiter was too quick for it. In less than an instant he had snatched up the goblet and, holding the bottle six inches away, let the wine foam into its cup, yellow and charged with bubbles. He set the glass once more before Mrs Clagg, returned the champagne to the bucket, shrouded with the napkin, just as Violet had so often seen it done on the films, said, 'To your good health, madam,' and disappeared. It was to Violet the most glorious and wonderful moment.

She sat for a few seconds contemplating the silvery bubbles leaping to the surface of the golden wine, and for the moment all the pieces of the day's shattered edifice reassembled themselves again. She was warm, about to be fed, dining in a restaurant car, and before her was her very own bottle of genuine champagne. She was a happy and contented woman.

She saw, then, that they were all watching her and waiting, and realised that since it was there she must taste and drink it. She almost wished, now that her great desire had been so generously fulfilled, that she didn't have to do so. The taste would be unfamiliar; she might not like it. If she didn't, three pairs of watchful eyes would know it at once.

She raised the glass to her lips, saying 'Cheers all!' and tasted it bravely. She didn't sip it timidly, but completed her initiation with a good hearty swallow.

She had not expected the acid taste, or the sting of the bubbles, but before her features could react to the unforeseen sourness the dose arrived at her middle, where it immediately set up its warm and friendly glow. Instead of a pucker a smile stole over the countenance of Violet Clagg.

'That's the stuff, eh, Mum?' said Will.

'Lovely,' said Violet.

The first wallop of gin had set up a similar glow in Granny's tummy. 'Really French, is it?' she asked.

Violet unveiled the bottle enough to peek at the label. 'It's from Reems,' she said, and then to all, 'Taste?'

Granny was the first to stick in a tentative tongue. She shook her head, 'I'll take me gin every time.'

'Oh, Mummy, I want to!' Gwendoline cried. No one protested; the glass was passed to her. She wet her lips with the liquid and made a face like the one Violet had wanted to at first. 'Ooh, ugh,' she said, 'sour,' and quickly got her nose back into the ginger-beer to get rid of the flavour.

Clagg laughed. 'What I say is, let 'em try it and then they won't be wanting it afterwards.'

Violet handed him the glass and he took a sip and wrinkled up his nose. 'Not a man's drink,' he said, and turned it back to her. Now it was all hers and hers alone. She knew its secret – sour at the top, warm and fuzzy inside. 'It's lovely,' she said once more. 'Cheers again!' She took a bigger swallow and was rewarded with an even greater glow.

A waiter arrived with food. 'Soup for the young lady?' he asked and prepared to set a dish before Gwendoline. Granny looked at him sharply. 'Why can't she have grapefruit?'

'Sorry, madam. Of course.'

The rest had soup. Gwendoline clapped her hands over her grapefruit, but when she tried it she made the same face as with the champagne. 'Ooh, ugh!' she cried again. 'Sour!'

'That's how you learn, young 'un,' her father said.

All of them had smiles on their faces now. The dinner was going to be a success.

*

It was just on midnight when Will Clagg inserted his key into the door of No. 56 Imperial Road, Little Pudney, and they trooped into the vestibule of the house, shutting the door behind them to be immediately overwhelmed by the silence that reigned there, an all-engulfing stillness through which the ticking of the clock on the mantelpiece sounded as startlingly loud as pistol-shots. Celebrations might still be going on elsewhere, but No. 56 Imperial Road was on the outlying fringe at the end of the bus-route and here everyone had gone to bed. There was not so much as the blat of a radio or the barking of a dog.

It was only then they realised that all through the long day their ear-drums had unceasingly been assaulted by noise and clamour.

There had been the sounds of the shuffling feet of spectators and the marching feet of men, the rolling thunder of military hardware, the roar of aircraft, blare of bands, shrill of fifes and keening of pipes. There had been train sounds, bus sounds, traffic sounds, the great roars of cheering, the clash of dishes from the jammed, packed restaurants they had tried to enter. Now the quiet was shocking in its intensity. To Will Clagg it sounded louder somehow than any of the uproar through which they had wandered that day, and to his surprise he found himself leading his family into their living-room almost on tiptoes.

They came in and sat down around the table, for it was also necessary for them to become re-acquainted with their own home, to relax in the security of its walls, to reopen themselves to its contours and its possessions. It seemed as though they had been away journeying through vast distances of space and time. They had been subjected to buffets and shocks of the mind as well as the body. They had suffered in spirit and had lived through a day more strange, and in a sense exciting too, than any dozen holidays at the sea could provide.

The little house in Imperial Road was the same as it had been when they left it – the worn carpet, the chair with the damaged leg, the Toby jug that Johnny had won at a fair, the photographs on the wall, the mantel clock and their own Coronation decorations, the red, white and blue paper ribbon criss-crossing the room from its four corners to the chandelier with the colour print of the Queen hanging over the fireplace. All was indeed the same, only they were not. They were changed drastically by what they had been through, and this was why they now found themselves sitting so uneasily and silently, a part of that great and surrounding quiet, trying to adjust themselves from the persons they had been to those they now were.

Violet Clagg was the first to re-enter the safe, snug cocoon of her home, the first to yield to the embrace of familiar things. She sighed and said, 'We'd better be getting the children to bed. Goodness knows how I'll ever be getting Johnny up and off to school in the morning.'

The boy cried, 'Oh, Mummy, do I *have* to go to school tomorrow?' His new and miraculous possession would be taking up so much of his time, giving him such a great deal to think about.

Before Granny could put her oar in, Clagg said, 'It's back to work for us all, m'lad.'

There was no appeal from his father, Johnny knew, and now the thought of school suddenly opened up heretofore unconsidered possibilities. He might let his best friends have just a glimpse of it. How envied he would be!

Granny said, 'I'll go and make us all a cup of tea.'

'See if there's a drop of gin left in the bottom of the bottle while you're at it, Granny,' Clagg suggested. 'You'll want something warming so you won't be catching your death of cold.' Granny went off quickly so that they wouldn't see her smile of satisfaction.

There had been no heat in the house for twenty-four hours of almost incessant rain, and it was chill, damp and clammy. Violet plugged in a small electric fire, set Gwenny before it and began to peel clothing from her, saying 'Get Gwenny's dressing-gown for her, Johnny, there's a good boy, and get yourself warm and snug as well.' Gwenny was dry enough; nevertheless her mother rubbed the little chest vigorously with her hand. Johnny returned, ready for bed, with his sister's wool robe.

Will Clagg said with a kind of studied casualness, 'Well now, Gwenny, you haven't told us yet what it was like seeing the Queen.' The fact was, he hadn't dared really to ask her up to that point. It had been nip and tuck as to whether she had got up on to the top of the barrier in time. He remembered the passage of the wave of cheering that accompanied what must have been her appearance, the sound of the coach horses with their outriders, and the rumble of the heavy coach. Had he lingered too long in surprise and bewilderment when the stranger, the little man, had told him to boost him up onto his shoulders? And once Gwenny was up, how quickly had she been able to grasp what she saw? There would have been a vast, confusing plain of heads and faces with the procession threading its way through like a river far away. Would the Queen already have passed by and entered the Park? Would all their endeavours thus have been totally in vain and the child disappointed? She had not mentioned the subject from the time she had come down from the wall.

Gwenny said, 'I saw her, Mummy, didn't I?'

'Yes, dear. That's what you said. But you never told us what she was like.'

With no change of expression whatsoever, Gwendoline retired instantly into that inner chamber to which children flee when cross-questioned what the party was like, and locked the door. Safe with her Queen no one could get at her. Her *alter ego*, which had to live with, put up with and get along with grown-ups, replied, 'She was lovely.'

Mrs. Clagg massaged the cold and clammy little feet. 'Of course. But what was she doing?'

The outside Gwenny said, 'She was riding in a golden coach, like Cinderella, drawn by eight white horses.'

Will Clagg's head came up. With one enormous inspiration he drew into his mighty chest almost all of the air in the room and exhaled it in one great sigh of relief. Perhaps, then, they really had been in time and had hoisted her to the barrier's top before the royal coach had passed from her view. He had managed to keep his promise to her.

Mrs. Clagg said, 'That's it, Gwenny, and what did she have on?'

Gwenny replied, 'A gold dress and a gold crown. And on the top of the gold crown was a gold butterfly. Its eyes were real diamonds and its wings were made of pearls.'

Her mother said, 'But, Gwenny, that's what the picture of the Butterfly Princess looks like in your fairy-tale book.'

Gwenny nodded in grave acquiescence. 'That's right,' she said.

Will Clagg's heart sank again. He asked, 'What else did you see, Gwenny?'

'The Prince was sitting next to her. He was dressed all in white. He blew me a kiss—'

Will and Violet Clagg exchanged glances and in them was recognition that comes to all parents that in the secret chambers of the minds of their children fact and fancy stand adjacent, and when questioned there was no telling over which threshold they would step before replying. Had she or had she not seen the Queen that day as she had so greatly desired? And if not, what then was it that she had seen? The conviction came to Will and Violet Clagg that they would probably never really know and that there was no use questioning her further.

Granny came in with the tea-tray, on which was also half a bottle of gin with three glasses and a few biscuits. Johnny's eyes brightened at the sight of the tea and biscuits and they all sat themselves down again around the table. The comfort of home was taking over and the discomforts and frustrations were already beginning to fade.

*

Each of them was cherishing the most extraordinary souvenirs that he or she had brought back from this day, which all the time it had been going on had appeared to be so disastrous, but now no longer seemed so. They had with their sacrifices made a gift to their young Queen and it was as if in return she had made an offering to each of them, one that none of them had expected.

Perhaps the strangest of all these benefactions was that which came to Granny as she sat there with her family. She was an old lady of seventy-three who had been through a day that was not only harrowing mentally, but trying and fatiguing physically. She had been rained on, trampled, jostled; she had been standing up hour upon hour and she felt extraordinarily well; as a matter of fact, had never felt better in her life.

Old people think about death. They are subject to ills and frailties and are reminded continually by their bodies that their days are numbered. Never, never would Granny, of course, let the family know what had been made manifest that day, namely the knowledge that she was a well preserved, healthy and sturdy person who would be around for a long time yet to keep an eye on things. It was as though she had received a doctor's verdict after a check-up: 'You're absolutely sound, Mrs Bonner, you'll live to be a hundred.'

She didn't want to live to be a hundred and be a burden, of course; she just wanted to live, to go on badgering Will, bossing her daughter, helping to bring up the children, watching them grow and develop. She wanted to go on eating, drinking, breathing and putting in her two pennies' worth until she grew tired. Somehow this day had told her that she would. It had soothed the secret and unspoken fears that had beset her. The grim mouth relaxed for a moment, almost into a smile, and the sharp eyes behind the spectacle lenses once more took in the familiar surroundings of the room. She would be there yet for quite a while.

As for Gwendoline, one would never know except that she was happy and satisfied. She hugged her secret to herself, whatever it was she had felt the need of and had found that day, as she would hug it to her heart for many months and years to come. Even when she was grown and her life and needs and desires changed there would still remain the residue of it all to warm her and to which she could return. Upon such small and hidden triumphs are sunny natures built.

Three weirdly assorted physical objects had been brought back from that journey of apparent fiasco: a newspaper cutting, a champagne cork and a polished military badge. Their intrinsic value was nil, and if you came upon them in an attic box, gathering dust, you would never guess or even begin to assess the meaning they had had in terms of human emotion, or suspect what symbols they were for ambition, love, pride, vanity and those hungers and yearnings of the soul which make us what we are.

Not until this total anonymity had been breached by those two lines of black type had Will Clagg ever dreamed that in his innermost person he had craved the sweets of celebrity. It had never dawned upon him to be worried over who he was or what he was, and much less what he was not. He awakened every morning and went through those rituals of washing and clothing himself and stoking his personal furnace with food to give him energy. He moved through space and time to his place of work where he was greeted with respect by those both beneath and above him. He did those things, gave those orders, took those precautions without which his unit would not operate properly. It was known as 'doing his job' and it was almost as automatic to him as breathing. His work done, his life then continued in its private train and he was himself, Will Clagg, friend or companion to other men of his station, husband and father and relation to his family, citizen and subject to his country and his Queen.

Still and all, it was a kind of oblivion, a facelessness. Now he had suddenly been plucked therefrom and existed as an entity outside of and far beyond the confines of Little Pudney.

He had become something apart, a person living upon another plane, entering and impinging upon, if even for an instant, the lives of all those who had read about him and his misadventure. It was as though he had been born again and therein he had found a joy and a sweetness undreamed of, and no less fulfilling because up to that point he had been unaware of its existence. If he had sacrificed with a full and generous heart, if he had suffered, he had indeed been well repaid.

In one hand Violet held her tea-cup, in the other she fondled the champagne cork she had carried away with her in her bag.

One might tie a tag to it: 'Souvenir of the Coronation', or 'Souvenir of one's first drink of champagne', or even 'Souvenir of something good happening'. For in a sense the cork represented the breaking of the pattern of disappointment in her life, things looked forward to which had not come off. True, she had not sat in the window and had wine poured by a butler, but instead it had been on a railway train in a restaurant car, something she had likewise never experienced before. But the bottle had been properly iced and napkin-wrapped, the waiter had worn a uniform, and had been kind and cheery and said, 'To your good health, madam'; and she had tasted and drunk champagne as she had craved to do.

But really the phrase with which Violet had tagged the

little cork she was turning over and over in her hand was quite a different one and she didn't know just how she had come upon it, but it sounded good to her and in her mind she wrote the ticket and tied it to the stopper: 'Souvenir of my husband's heart'.

For love was something of which Violet Clagg had not thought for a long time. Will, of course, had once told her he loved her when they were young. They had married and had children. They were not of that breed habituated to interminable reiteration of passion and affection; neither would have dreamed of asking of the other: 'Do you love me?' It would have embarrassed them to death. They still came together occasionally out of necessity or desire, or a moment's flare-up of passion, and Clagg sometimes looked upon her fondly or patted her hand and called her 'old girl'. But, of course, of those evidences of the 'love' of poets, or the more visual one of the cinema, – the moonlight walks with arms about waists, the whispered avowals and protestations, the sighs and glances and stammerings – there were no more, nor was it to be expected. Where then was this love? What had become of that which once had been whispered between them! Why, it was in that champagne cork, now so warm and moist from the contact of her hand.

It spoke, it shouted, it sang to her all the words and songs that her husband could never utter. He thought about her. Her place in his heart was secure. Her happiness, the fulfilment of a wish or dream of hers that lay within his power was of importance to him. He had remembered! He loved her! She would never forget this Coronation day.

Johnny sat with both hands beneath the fringed chenille table-cloth. His fingers for the hundredth time were memorising the contours of the badge, the crown, the lion, the unicorn, and the word *FIDELIS*. The dream now had taken on an altered quality. Some of the childishness and exaggeration had departed from it. The words of the old gentleman came back to him 'never relent!' He was looking ahead and beginning to concentrate upon his future. Some day he would wear that insignia by right. He had begun to grow up.

*

Granny poured another cup of tea for all of them, heavily sugared for the children, with plenty of milk. Will Clagg measured out a generous portion of gin into each of the three glasses for Granny, Violet and himself. They were all there, safe, sound and snug, and he felt that the occasion called for a speech, and he gathered his resources together to make it. In some subtle way he had been re-established as head of the family, his person and authority once more looked up to. He eyed them gravely and cleared his throat to let them know he was about to say something, and was rewarded with satisfactory silence and attention.

'Well,' he began, 'it has been quite a day.' He wondered how it was possible for a man to have so many hundreds of thoughts coursing through his head and yet be able to express so little. To have to sum up all that he had felt about paying homage to his Queen, the strange love that had stirred in him, and all the emotions he had felt in one sentence – 'Well, it has been quite a day'.

'It didn't turn out quite as we expected,' he continued, 'but then we went, didn't we? We tried.'

Clagg's mind suddenly leaped to the newspaper cutting in his wallet and he said, 'If the Queen reads the newspapers, as I'm sure she does, she'll know that we tried because what happened to us was written up there. But it doesn't matter what happened to us. It isn't us that counts on a day like this, it's her, and thank God all went well. So we ought to drink a toast to her, and then go to bed.'

There were no disagreements. Johnny was thinking it would be wonderful to be able to make a speech like that, and hoped that some day he could do the same.

Clagg raised his glass of gin in the direction of the coloured photograph over the mantlepiece and proposed 'To Her Majesty, Queen Elizabeth the Second. God save and bless her!' The two women lifted their glasses likewise.

'Wait a minute,' said Will Clagg, and with a spoon he tipped a few drops of gin into the tea-cups of his son and daughter.

'There now,' he said. 'Properly! All of us!'

*